The Missing Link

The Missing Link

Sheila Parker

*Blackie & Co
Publishers Ltd*

A BLACKIE & CO PUBLISHERS PAPERBACK

© Copyright 2002
Sheila Parker

The right of Sheila Parker to be identified as the author of
this work has been asserted by her in accordance with the
Copyright, Designs and Patents Act 1988

First published in 2002

A CIP catalogue record for this title is
available from the British Library

ISBN 1 903138 84 1

Blackie & Co Publishers Ltd
107-111 Fleet Street
LONDON EC4A 2AB

Acknowledgements

With my grateful thanks to my family for their support and encouragement, and to my relatives, friends and others who have helped me in my research for this book.

I would also like to thank Bettina Croft for her kindness, guidance and support.

Bought on our Holiday Guernsey / Cann 2007 Patricia

THE MISSING LINK
(PROLOGUE)

The door bell rang as Laurence Morgan reached for the marmalade and glancing across the table he told his wife, 'It's probably one of the neighbours wanting to borrow something.'

'I don't believe in that sort of thing. I've never done it before and I'm not going to start now.' Although it was only eight-fifteen Margaret was bad mood and Laurence was thank-ful he would be at work all day. Margaret made no attempt to move, deliberately biting into her toast and chewing it slowly when the bell rang again.

Laurence stood up, at the same time picking up his jacket which was draped over the back of his chair. 'I haven't finished my breakfast however I'll answer it so you can enjoy yours.'

The shadow of two uniformed figures through the smoke glass panels of the front door brought a frown to Laurence's round and usually good-humoured face. On opening the door he immediately noticed the sombre expressions of the sergeant and W.P.C. 'Mr. Morgan, Mr. Laurence Morgan?' enquired the W.P.C. while the sergeant said, 'I'm afraid we have some bad news. Can we come in, sir.'

'Yes, of course.'

'What's happened? Why are the police here?' asked Margaret a moment later as she followed Laurence into the living room.

'I regret that we're the bearer of sad news, Mrs. Morgan' said the sergeant.

'What have you been doing?' Margaret glared at Laurence who shook his head when she continued, 'It can't be anything to do with Keith. He's in the kitchen having his breakfast, besides he's only five so I can't see ....'

'Please, Mrs. Morgan' remonstrated the sergeant who then turned to Laurence. 'I understand Richard Gilmour-Morgan, the concert pianist, is your brother.'

'Yes' and as he met the sergeant's direct gaze Laurence burst out, 'You're trying to tell me something's happened to him.'

The sergeant nodded. 'Mr. Morgan, his wife and the driver of their car were all killed when an articulated lorry crashed ...'

Laurence shuddered and buried his face in his hands. 'Oh God, no! It can't be true.'

The W.P.C. who had been ready to comfort Margaret but was seated beside Laurence on the settee now placed her hand on his arm. 'I'm sorry, sir.'

'Where .. when did this happen?' asked Laurence and without pausing for breath, 'Oh my God, the children' and his gaze travelling from the WPC to the sergeant, 'Has Susan, their Nanny been told?'

'No. It was decided that you should be the first to know.' Although the WPC already knew that Richard and Irene Morgan were the parents of triplets, three little girls, she enquired, 'How old are they?'

'Eighteen months. There's three of them, all lovely little girls. It's difficult to know which is which.'

The WPC'S gaze flickered towards Margaret Morgan, whose expression was forbidding rather than shocked. She had not uttered a word of compassion or even glanced at her husband, who was now shivering. 'How am I going to tell Susan?'

Disgusted at the lack of response from Mrs. Morgan the WPC stood up and moved across the room. 'I'm sure we could all drink a cup of tea.'

In a flash Margaret was on her feet, rudely pushing past the young police woman. 'I'm quite capable of doing that. There's no need for you to go snooping in my kitchen.'

The WPC noted the sergeant's eye-brows twitch as he turned towards Laurence. 'Obviously the nanny is resident and expecting her employers to return some time this morning.'

'Yes.' Laurence blinked and forced himself to speak slowly. 'On occasions Irene and Richard stayed overnight with friends in London but if it was an early concert they'd come home. I don't know who was with them last night.' Laurence gazed at the WPC who was again sitting beside him, her hand on his arm and he repeated, 'How am I going to tell Susan?'

'We'll be with you' she told him and still in a gentle voice, 'Do you have any other relatives, or will you and your wife stay there while arrangements are being made?'

'What arrangements?' demanded Margaret suddenly appearing in the doorway and before anyone could answer she stared at Laurence, 'Are you going in to work today, and what about taking Keith to school?'

'Of course I'm not going to work. There are other more important matters that require my attention and Keith can come with us, see his cousins ...' Laurence's voice faded under his wife's baleful glare. 'I'll phone the office in a moment.'

'I'll do that for you' offered the WPC while Margaret snorted ungraciously and muttered something about fetching the tea.

During the few minutes they were alone the sergeant learnt that there were no other relatives and it was quite unlikely that the other god-parents were available. Laurence knew that one of them, Heather Wingate, was abroad with her husband who was currently U.N. Resident Representative for Indonesia and Margaret, (his wife) was god-mother to Tessa.

'Poor children' muttered the sergeant under his breath and then asked, 'Are Irene Morgan's parents still alive?'

'Mr. and Mrs. Taylor. Yes, they live in Scotland, somewhere near Stirling. Unfortunately neither of them enjoy good health. I doubt that they could cope with the journey, or the trauma of the funeral.' As he uttered those words Laurence looked at the sergeant. 'When will I be able to make the necessary arrangements?'

'Not yet. Certain formalities will have to be completed but I'm sure some of your brother's friends will be very supportive.'

Some time later Susan gazed at Laurence with tear- filled eyes and whispered, 'I can't believe it. They're both dead?'

'I'm afraid so, my dear. And the person who accompanied them.'

'That was Irene's friend, Felicity. She usually drives.' Susan covered her mouth as she spoke, her voice barely audible. 'It wasn't her fault, was it?'

'No my dear, it wasn't.' Laurence and Susan both turned to look at the three little girls who sat on the floor with the WPC, reaching out to touch her silver buttons as she quietly told them a story of her own invention.

'What's going to happen?' whispered Susan.

'I haven't had time to think.' Laurence had been disgusted that, for no good reason, Margaret had refused to accompany him and he had been grateful for the WPC's support. He now nodded with gratitude and approval as Susan told him that, with the help of the housekeeper, who was also very fond of the children, she could manage for a few days. Her distress still very evident Susan then asked, 'Will you come and live here?'

'I've really no idea, my dear.'

'I'm sure Mrs. Morgan will want to do whatever is best for the children' offered Susan, unaware that the WPC had looked up at her with a doubtful expression.

On her return to the station the WPC informed the sergeant of Susan's composure. 'She was quite remarkable, really loves those children and is genuinely concerned about their future. That's more than you can say about Margaret Morgan. You must have noticed she didn't utter a word of sympathy or compassion. I felt so sorry for Laurence when Susan asked about the children's future. With a wife like his he probably didn't know what to say.'

'Stop worrying about them. I'm sure he's capable of making the right decision.'

'I can't help it. They're such lovely and happy toddlers - Tessa, Jessica and Amanda - you can't help loving them.' The WPC gave a wistful sigh. 'I wonder what will become of them?'

CHAPTER ONE

'Jessica! How....?'

Amanda Lockwood was spun round in the middle of the pedestrian crossing by the tall man who had been staring at her from the other side of South Street. Although he was a complete stranger she was alarmed by his sudden pallor and expression, and allowed him to propel her back to where she had started.

As soon as they reached the pavement and disregarding the passers-by the man, who was now shaking, said hoarsely, 'It's impossible, the.. the accident was ten days ago. You can't be Jessica.'

'I'm not, and I've no idea who she is.' Amanda gazed at the fair haired man with concern, under normal circumstances she would have considered him handsome but now he was almost haggard and staring at her, wide-eyed. Amanda knew that if this had happened at home, in Guernsey, other people would have also offered their help but here in Exeter everyone went about their own business. She had often been told by her husband, who was a policeman, that she shouldn't enter into conversation with complete strangers but now she said, 'You're ill. Can I get you a taxi to take you home or to your hotel?'

'No thank you. I'll be fine in a minute. It's the shock. Could we go somewhere for tea so I can apologise and explain. '

'There's a hotel over-looking the cathedral, not far from here' suggested Amanda as she studied the pale features, noting the smart pin-striped suit, white shirt and dark blue silk tie. 'Will you be able to walk there?' They were standing on the corner of High Street and South Street.

'Yes. I know where you mean.'

1

'I still can't think straight. I don't know where to start' said Matthew Ormerod as they sat in the residents lounge, waiting. Tea and biscuits had been ordered.

They had exchanged names whilst walking and relieved that her companion had stopped shaking Amanda ventured, 'You thought I was someone else.'

'Yes, my sister-in-law. She's, or rather was, Tessa's twin. Tessa is my wife. They were identical but unfortunately Jessica died ten days ago as a result of a car accident. Something was wrong with the brakes and the police are now making enquiries. In spite of this I thought you were Jessica.'

'Everyone is supposed to have a double' said Amanda pouring tea, and pushing the plate of biscuits towards Matthew and then helping herself.

'It's .. it's more than that.' Matthew drank his tea quickly and shook his head. 'Your voice and facial expressions are exactly the same as Tessa's and Jessica's. Could you be related - distant cousins, something like that? I'm sure Tessa will want to know more about you.' Matthew felt inside his jacket, 'I usually carry some photographs but I must have left them in my hotel bedroom, on the bedside table. Why don't we have a drink together this evening, then you can see the likeness for yourself. In the meantime I'll 'phone Tessa and you can tell your husband.'

Amanda could hear her husband's warning voice, 'Don't be silly. You know nothing about this man. It could all be a ploy' and stood up. 'I don't see how we could possibly be related. I live in Guernsey, in the Channel Islands. I don't have any relatives in England.'

'I'm sorry, I didn't mean to upset you. Can I see you back to your hotel, or organise a taxi?'

'There's no need for either, thank you. I'm staying at The White Hart, at the bottom of South Street so I haven't far to go.'

2

It was as they reached the main entrance that a short, portly gentleman stopped abruptly and exclaimed, 'Matthew, Tessa! It's lovely to see you both, especially you Tessa. I knew Matthew was driving down to look at the contents of Oakdene House. Have you both been out there? Are there any pieces you'd like for the shop?' And without pausing for breath, 'How are you, my dear?'

Matthew opened his mouth but it was Amanda who spoke. 'I'm sorry to mislead you but I'm not Tessa. I'm Amanda Lockwood, from Guernsey. Mr. Ormerod thought I was Jessica and is just recovering from the shock.'

Amanda looked concerned again as Matthews helped the newcomer to a nearby chair and told her not to worry. 'I'm sure he'll be fine in a moment' and then hurriedly added, 'Sorry I should have introduced you, this is my uncle, Benjamin Ormerod.'

'I'm sorry I've upset you.' Amanda smiled at the round-faced gentleman as she spoke. 'My presence in Exeter is certainly causing some confusion.'

'It's not your fault, my dear. I must say the likeness is incredible, and your voice is exactly the same.' Then, turning to Matthew, 'Stop fussing over me, I'm fine. It was just the shock seeing you and a lovely young woman whom I really thought was Tessa, and then I learn she isn't. You could certainly have fooled me.'

'That's the last thing I'd ever do but perhaps you can help me, Uncle Ben. I'm trying to persuade Amanda to join me for a drink this evening so I can show her the photographs of Tessa.'

'Good idea!' Ben Ormerod was now standing and gazing at Amanda, his colour restored. 'You must be wondering what I was talking about. Matthew has an antique shop in Bristol, hence his visit to Oakdene House, a large country house some three miles south of Exeter. The contents, most of which are genuine antiques, are to be auctioned in the morning. Tessa is also very knowledgeable about antiques, in fact she's on the Antique Road Show team, and often accompanies Matthew on such visits.'

'I'm afraid that although I'm very interested in antiques, I don't know very much about them, but it all sounds very interesting.'

'It is. Although Matthew now runs what was the family business I often pop in to see him. But enough about all that. I'm staying here overnight so if you're free this evening, why not join us for a drink when you can see Matthew's photos and tell us more about yourself. I'm sure Tessa, who is naturally still very upset, will be very interested to hear all about you.'

'Where were your parents living when they adopted you?' enquired Uncle Ben.

'In Bath.' As she changed to meet Matthew and his uncle Amanda had thought about this and decided that, although she had been adopted it was highly unlikely that there could be any connection between Tessa, Jessica and herself. 'We lived on the outskirts and I had a very happy childhood whilst we were there. However my parents were both keen to move when the opportunity occurred to go to Guernsey. We all flew over when Dad had his interview and thought it was a lovely island. I was due to start at another school in the September however I'm sure you don't want to hear about this.'

'Oh yes we do, my dear.' Ben noted that, once again, Matthew was gazing at Amanda intensely. 'I'm sure Tessa won't stop asking questions.'

Amanda had refrained from asking about Tessa but her curiosity increased as Matthew extracted two photographs from his wallet and her expression was one of incredulity as her gaze travelled from that of Matthew and Tessa, to one of

Tessa and Jessica. Unconsciously her lips curved into an identical smile when Matthew jumped up, pulled Amanda to her feet and indicating her reflection in the mirror on the opposite wall said, 'Look! You can see for yourself that, apart from your hair style, your features and colouring are very similar. You've already told us that you were adopted, could you possibly be related?'

'I don't know and, before you ask, I've never tried to trace my natural parents. I wouldn't want to hurt my adoptive parents who have always been wonderful to me. However, I must go.'

'No, not yet' said Matthew while Uncle Ben said, 'I'm not keen on eating a solitary dinner. Why don't we all dine here?'

'Uncle Ben, you're a genius!' Matthew turned to Amanda, grinning, 'If I promise not to ask any more questions, will you join us?'

Amanda hesitated. Up to now she had suppressed her curiosity and she now said, 'Thank you. I would like to know more about Tessa and Jessica.'

It was three hours later, back in her hotel bedroom, that Amanda stared in the mirror noting her flushed cheeks, and ran her fingers through her hair. Her thoughts were still in a whirl.

During the evening she had learnt that after losing their parents in a car accident Tessa and Jessica had been brought up by an aunt and uncle. They were only eighteen months old at the time, and she had been adopted at the same age. She had been told about this when she was seven years old.

Within minutes Amanda was ready for bed when she murmured, 'It all happened the same year.' Her head on the pillow, her eyes closed, Amanda was still wondering what Tessa's reaction would be when Matthew told her. But, more important, how would her parents and Tim react? Could she possibly be related to Tessa and Jessica, and what was so suspicious about Jessica's death?

Meanwhile, Ben Ormerod, relaxed in a comfortable armchair in his bedroom, was reflecting that it had been an enlightening evening. His gaze had constantly travelled from Matthew to Amanda and, at the same time, he had noted the inflection in her voice when she spoke of her husband, her parents and her love of music. On learning that she was music teacher at one of the island schools he and Matthew had exchanged glances but neither had commented. They both knew that, as children, Tessa and Jessica were interested in music but piano and singing lessons had been discouraged by their Aunt Margaret.

Ben reached for the bottle of malt whisky and poured himself another drink recalling Jessica's delight when Roger's mother gave her a piano as a personal wedding present.

Ben considered that Jessica had also been fortunate to have a supportive mother-in-law. Olivia Bostock had soon discovered that Jessica possessed a fine soprano voice and persuaded her that she should join the local amateur and dramatic society. Tessa had been thrilled to hear of Olivia's suggestion and told Jessica that she should not miss this opportunity. Ben closed his eyes but not to sleep, instead he visualised the first production in which Jessica appeared. Although she only had a minor role there were occasions when her voice soared above the others when Ben had noted murmurs of approval from the audience seated nearby. It had taken him back to the days when he heard Irene, Jessica's mother, sing and he was happy that one of the girls had inherited this gift. He had also shared Tessa's and Roger's delight at the review in the local paper. The reporter, a crotchety middle-aged man, had praised everything about the production, noted that there was a newcomer with a fine voice and hoped that more would be heard of her in the future.

His eyes still closed Ben reflected that Margaret and Laurence had been unkind and inconsiderate in not telling Tessa and Jessica that their parents had both been well-known in the music world until they were twelve. Ben had never heard either of the girls criticise their aunt and uncle but from various remarks made by them on different occasions it was obvious that their childhood had not been particularly happy. And now Jessica's untimely death had brought Tessa more unhappiness.

Although his friend, Jim Fowler, who a Detective Chief Inspector, was in charge of the case, had promised to keep him advised of any developments, Ben had not heard from him for several days and decided to ring Jim first thing in the morning.

CHAPTER TWO

'It's impossible! How could we be related?' Tessa's eyes had widened with incredulity as Matthew recounted the events of the previous afternoon and evening. 'Everyone is supposed to have a double and it was coincidence that you met mine.'

'Amanda's voice is like yours, possibly slightly lower and, although it's longer, her hair-style is similar' persisted Matthew. Then, producing a photograph from his breast pocket he handed it to Tessa, 'Have a look at this.'

Tessa frowned and shook her head. 'When did you take this? I don't remember seeing it before.'

'You wouldn't, it's not you. That's Amanda Lockwood. Uncle Ben took it last night and had the film developed this morning.' Matthew could see that Tessa was bewildered and at a loss for words. 'Uncle Ben mistook her for you in the first place, and was as astonished as me. As you know he always takes his camera wherever he goes, and this was an opportunity not to be missed.'

'I realise I keep repeating myself but it's incredible. I could be looking at a photo of myself or Jessica.' Tessa turned to look at Matthew, 'You learnt quite a lot about Amanda in a short time and now I must admit I'm curious to know even more about her.' Tessa's voice faded but after a moment she resumed, 'I wonder what Jessica would have said or done if she'd seen this?'

'She'd probably have been just as curious as you are.' Matthew drank the remainder of his tea, then pushed the cup and saucer aside. 'Did your aunt or uncle ever talk about any relatives?'

'No. They hardly ever spoke about our parents. Uncle Laurence tried on numerous occasions but Aunt Margaret always butted in. Told him to get on with different jobs. Poor Uncle Laurence, he was really henpecked. I don't think he had an easy life.' Tessa's eyes misted over. 'We only knew they died in a car accident and Uncle Laurence never spoke of any other brothers or sisters. He was kind to us, interested in our education but whenever he tried to spend some time with us Aunt Margaret, or that horrible Keith - and I don't think he's changed - wanted him to do something else.'

Matthew moved to the settee and pulled Tessa close. 'My poor love. You did have a rotten time, didn't you?'

'It made Jess .. Jessica and I even closer but, in spite of that, it always seemed as though there was something missing. As we grew older we used to discuss Aunt Margaret's attitude towards us. She may have been fond of us but there were never any hugs or kisses. At times we thought she wanted to tell us something but changed her mind.'

Matthew knew that they were twelve when Margaret told them their father had been a well-known concert pianist and their mother a singer but despite this he said, 'Perhaps it was about your parents.'

Tessa looked wistful. 'If it was about them I'll never know but it was marvellous to know that Uncle Ben had attended some of the concerts, even met them. He and Roger's mother have been very kind to bo.. both of us, telling us about the different concerts they'd attended.' Tessa paused and still holding Matthew's hand continued, 'Did Amanda ask any questions about me? Could she come back to England again, so we can meet?'

'She certainly wanted to know more about you.' Matthew hesitated, he didn't want Tessa to be disappointed if Amanda didn't share her enthusiasm about meeting. He knew that Tessa missed Jessica, although they only met once a week hardly a day passed when there wasn't a 'phone call. 'As far as meeting is concerned, Amanda will probably have to wait until the school holidays. She teaches music.' Matthew was pleased to see Tessa's eyes light up with interest and curiosity, and concluded 'the piano. Apparently Amanda's adoptive parents were very supportive and encouraging when she was young and showed an interest in music.'

'So we both have the same interest' said Tessa softly and looking at Matthew, 'If Amanda can't come here why don't we fly over to Guernsey for a long week-end.' Tessa nodded as Matthew pointed out that Amanda might not be so eager but despite this she continued, 'We've never been to the island so if she and I didn't like each other, then we could have a short holiday. You've been working very hard lately, it would do you good to have a break.'

'Let's wait and see.'

Meanwhile, in Guernsey, a similar conversation was taking place. Amanda had returned from Exeter that morning but it was now late afternoon and she was recounting the events of the previous day. Timothy's expression had grown more amazed as Amanda continued, nevertheless he listened without interruption. At last Amanda concluded, 'We know I was adopted, so do you think I could be related to Tessa?'

'I suppose it's possible. Your parents may be able to help you.'

Amanda's expression became serious. 'I don't want to hurt their feelings.' Then, as the idea occurred to her, 'Surely I wouldn't have been adopted if there had been any close relatives. Anyhow I'll have a chat with Mum and Dad tomorrow' and when Tim looked puzzled Amanda reminded him that they were all going to a concert at St. James.

Although it was a week old and she had read the news item several times Susan Ratcliffe picked up The Evening Post again. At first she couldn't believe that Jessica, one of the triplets who had been in her charge so many years ago, was dead. The account in the paper stated that she had been killed in a car accident, possibly due to brake failure and that the police were investigating.

Twenty-five years had elapsed since Susan looked after Jessica, Tessa and Amanda but despite this length of time she had never forgotten them. She had written to their aunt, Margaret Morgan, enquiring about them on several occasions but had never received a reply and gradually reconciled herself to the fact that Margaret was too busy caring for the children to write letters.

An avid reader of The Evening Post Susan had almost shouted with joy on seeing Jessica's wedding photograph and immediately cut this out, placing it with her few souvenirs of the time she had worked for the Gilmour-Morgans. It was the double-barrelled name which had attracted her attention to the photograph in the first place and again, six months later, when Tessa was married. On both occasions she had wanted to write to the young brides but her husband Bob had dissuaded her, pointing out that too many years had elapsed. They would have been too young to remember her.

During the last twelve months she had scanned the paper, thinking that Amanda would probably be getting married but this had not happened. Instead she had recently read the account of Jessica's death and, blinking back her tears, Susan resolved that she would write to Tessa and reached for her writing paper. She knew Tessa's married name from the cutting and had already found the address in the telephone directory but for a brief moment Susan recalled the two worse mornings in her life. The first had been when Laurence and the WPC had called to inform her that her employers, Richard and Irene Gilmour-Morgan, the triplets' parents, had died in a car crash. The second was also devastating. Margaret Morgan's announcement that she would not require Susan's services had been made scarcely a week after the accident when Susan had been heart-broken. She knew the Morgan's house wasn't large enough to accommodate the triplets and herself and, in the interim, Margaret had intimated that although Richard's house was larger, she had no intention of moving. Nevertheless it was a terrible shock.

From the morning that he was informed of his brother's death Laurence had been a daily visitor, calling in for a few minutes on his way to work and again late afternoon, for half an hour, when Susan had been pleased to see him. She could still remember how embarrassed and apologetic Laurence had been when he kissed her on the cheek, and wished her good luck. He had personally written an excellent reference and, after spending a fortnight at home with her parents, Susan had taken a position as nanny to a two year old boy and four year old girl whose parents owned a hotel in Shepton Mallet.

It was there that she met and fell in love with Bob, her employer's brother. They were married two years later. Although she soon had children of her own she had often thought of her previous charges, disappointed that her letters enquiring about them had been ignored. At the time she thought that if Margaret was too busy Laurence might reply but considered that her letters had been pushed aside, and he knew nothing about them.

A few minutes later, as she slid the letter into an envelope, Susan wondered if Tessa was as fortunate as she had been, marrying into an affectionate and caring family. Her in-laws always greeted her parents with affection and enthusiasm when they came to see the grandchildren, and encouraged them to extend their visits.

As the children grew up Susan was amazed that it was they who were interested in the different aspects of running a hotel, rather than her niece and nephew. Colin, her brother-in-law, had been delighted about this and whilst he and Bob encouraged their interest, neither had been pushed, with the result that Fiona was working in Reception while Daniel was at a hotel school in Austria.

Although Susan had been engaged to look after Doris' children the two women had taken an instant liking to each other and become good friends. Susan smiled as she recalled that Doris had always encouraged her to talk about the triplets. It was after Fiona and Daniel had reached school age that Doris spoke of a problem that had been troubling Colin and Bob for some time. On learning that some of the young mothers working at the hotel were anxious to keep their jobs but were experiencing difficulty in finding a suitable person to care for their young children, Susan agreed that she would look after the three youngsters in question: a boy aged two, and two girls aged three and three and a half, who were friends, for four mornings a week. Over the years these had been replaced by others and all the mothers had praised Susan for the care and affection she gave their children.

'How lovely to see you! I've only just made a pot of tea.' Doris' round face was wreathed in smiles as she hugged Susan and then led her to a comfortable but cluttered living room which faced the patio and garden. A short plump woman, her brown hair graying at the temples, Doris was gregarious and Susan had scarcely sat down when Doris asked, 'Have you thought any more about writing to Tessa?' She had known of Susan's intention to do this and nodded encouragingly when she heard that the letter had been posted. 'I'm sure she'll be delighted to hear from you. You're probably the only person who knew her parents.'

'Yes, and they were a lovely couple. They were so happy with their three little girls and I enjoyed working for them. They were very kind to me. I must admit it was very hectic at first but Irene was happy with the routine I suggested. She had arranged that she wouldn't accept any engagements for the first twelve months and we worked very well together.' Doris and her husband, both music lovers, had been amazed that Susan had worked for Richard and Irene Gilmour-Morgan, and sadly admitted that they had only attended one concert.

Over the years Susan had spoken of the triplets on numerous occasions but this did not prevent Doris from saying, 'I know I've asked you this before but I can't remember your answer. How did you know which was which?'

'When they came home they had different coloured arm bands then, after a while, we noticed moles in different places on their arms. These were not unsightly and Irene considered it could be an ideal way of identifying them. They were already fiddling with their arm bands but Irene thought it as well to use them until they were older, when other features might become visible.' Susan paused and looked wistful. 'I didn't have the opportunity to tell Margaret Morgan about their moles however I'm sure she coped very capably. Laurence probably helped when he was home and possibly Keith, although he was a rather obnoxious five year old at the time.'

'Poor little mites losing both their parents.' Doris sighed, 'I hope they had a happy childhood in spite of that. Perhaps Tessa will tell you all about it.'

'If she replies' said Susan.

CHAPTER THREE

'It's very good of you to spare the time, Jim,' said Ben Ormerod after he and Detective Chief Inspector Fowler had shaken hands and seated themselves at the corner table. Jim glanced around the restaurant, noting the spaciousness, subtle but pleasing decor, sparkling glasses, gleaming cutlery and apple green tablecloths and matching serviettes. 'This is all very new, isn't it?'

'Yes. The restaurant has recently changed hands but I've heard that the food is very good. I thought this would be a good opportunity to sample it.'

The two men accepted proffered menus and after a few minutes studying these, food and wine ordered, Jim said 'I'm sure you're wondering what, if any, progress has been made into Jessica's death.'

Ben nodded. 'I must admit I am. Although I didn't know Jessica as well as Tessa, I keep asking myself why?'

'Unfortunately we gleaned very little from her colleagues at the estate agency or her friends, who all spoke of her with love and respect. We've yet to discover if any of them had a motive. They all knew that Jessica drove a Metro which, unlike new cars, did not indicate any brake deficiency.'

Jim paused while their plates were removed, the dessert menu declined, and coffee ordered. 'The agency car was in for service so Jessica was using her own car which meant that it was in the space behind the agency during the afternoon, (she had used it to meet clients on the Friday morning) and in her own carport during the evening and overnight. Both areas were easily accessible....'

'But surely one of the staff would have noticed ..' Ben stopped abruptly as Jim shook his head and told him that, apart from the toilet, there were no windows facing that direction. Ben also learnt that staff from the neighbouring shops and offices had not seen anyone loitering in or near the agency parking area, neither had the neighbours seen any strangers near Bostock's carport or drive-way during the evening or early morning.

'If Jessica hadn't driven out to Chew Valley to show those clients that particular property the accident wouldn't have happened.' Ben paused as the coffee was poured and then resumed, 'They had to drive down Blackboy Hill on their way from Henleaze, where they live, to the agency so why didn't she discover there was something wrong with the brakes?'

'Roger drove in and, when questioned, said there was no reason for him to use the brakes,' replied Jim.

'Did anyone else, apart from the staff, know where Jessica was going that morning, and which route she would be taking?'

'Yes, they all knew she was going to meet Mr. and Mrs. Baker at the house, which faces Chew Valley lake. Apparently Jessica had shown these clients other properties that didn't suit them. Mrs. Baker was very upset when a policeman went to the house, where they were waiting, to tell them the reason why Jessica hadn't turned up.'

'I realise I've questioned you before about your sister and I don't want to upset you unnecessarily Mrs. Ormerod, however I'm hoping you might be able to tell me something else which might help us with our enquiries.'

Chief Inspector Fowler had questioned Roger Bostock and Gregory Niven earlier that afternoon, soon after lunch with his old friend, Ben Ormerod, and now gazed at Tessa. Although he knew that she and Jessica were an identical twin once again he was amazed at the incredible likeness. Apart from scratches and bruises Jessica had not suffered any severe facial injuries, - how this had been achieved neither the doctor at the scene nor the pathologist could fathom - and he could still see the expression of horror on her face. Their hair was the colour of burnished copper and Jessica had worn hers slightly longer, curling just below her ears.

Tessa ran her fingers through her short curls and her sapphire blue eyes met his. 'What exactly do you want to know, Chief Inspector?'

'I've heard that twins are usually very close, did your sister ever tell you if there were any disagreements or arguments between any of her friends or colleagues at work, and herself?'

'No. Neither of us have a large circle of friends but we've always remained on good terms with those we do have.'

'What about previous men friends, - relationships? Did they end amicably?' Fowler knew that Jessica and Gregory Niven had been very friendly prior to Roger joining the agency, their immediate interest in each other and subsequent marriage.

'Yes.'

Tessa then said that Jessica hadn't spoken of any difficulties, and that Gregory hadn't shown any signs of jealousy or resentment at the wedding.

'So they all worked together amicably?' persisted Fowler.

'I've already told you that.' Tessa did not attempt to hide her impatience. 'I'm sorry, Chief Inspector, I've answered all these questions before and I fail to see that this conversation is of any help to you.'

'But it is, Mrs. Ormerod. Now, how well do you know Gregory Niven?'

In reply to this and other questions Fowler learnt that Tessa did not know Gregory very well. She had met him on various occasions when he called for Jessica and, a considerable time later, at the wedding, which he attended alone. Tessa also told him that Jessica had never spoken about

Gregory at any length since her marriage and concluded, 'As you already know Jessica enjoyed her work, - meeting different people, viewing properties and negotiating terms of sale.'

'Thank you, Mrs. Ormerod, you've been very helpful. I'll be in touch as soon as there's any news.'

'I can't believe, understand how such a terrible thing could happen...' Tessa stopped abruptly and blew her nose. They were now standing in the hall as Tessa gazed up at the Chief Inspector, who was 6'3" and considerably taller than herself.

Driving back to the station Fowler considered that although Tessa had naturally been devastated at Jessica's death, she had struggled to remain calm and dry-eyed when he had expected tears. At the inquest her expression had been strained, her face pale but she had again remained dry-eyed and was obviously relieved that Jessica's body was released for burial. Even at the funeral, Fowler had seated himself at the back of the church and later distanced himself from the graveside, there had been no stormy outburst but a trickle of tears as she clutched Matthew's hand.

Fowler's thoughts then turned to Roger and Gregory Niven again. Roger's mother had been at his side at the funeral, quietly weeping at the loss of her daughter-in-law and it was Roger, although pale and distraught, who had comforted her. It was only natural that Roger should be distressed and bewildered at Jessica's tragic death but Fowler still considered it strange that Gregory, who was now only her employer, had been so devastated. Was he still in love with Jessica?

Back in his office and seated at his desk Fowler was glad to be alone, he had told Detective Sergeant Branch (who had been with him when they called on Roger and Gregory) to go home and now considered those named in Jessica's Will. There were no children and the two main beneficiaries were Roger and Tessa, however the former had inherited the house and a considerable sum of money from his paternal grandparents and was the only child of a wealthy widow while Tessa, like Jessica, had received a substantial legacy from their maternal grandparents, on her twenty-first birthday.

Fowler's thoughts then turned to those who were to receive smaller bequests. Pauline Yates, a school friend whose husband had left her with a six months old baby whilst Romayne Wallis, another school friend, was a widow with two young children. Although Roger had never met Pauline or Romayne he knew about them and was able to produce recent letters in which they both expressed their appreciation for the money that Jessica had sent them. Fowler had also learnt that, whilst Jessica had not received any letters or 'phone calls asking for financial help, she had sent both friends money regularly. Reading their letters Fowler noted that there was no way either could be responsible for Jessica's death. Pauline lived with an elderly aunt near Malvern whilst Romayne lived in Leicester and neither had any means of transport. Jessica's bequests would therefore be a godsend to both of them.

Keith Morgan, the only son of Margaret and Laurence Morgan with whom Jessica and Tessa had lived until they were eighteen, was Jessica's only relative, however he was not mentioned in her Will.

CHAPTER FOUR

Hazel and Bruce Maybury held hands, their gaze on Amanda as, never faltering, she recalled her encounter with Matthew Ormerod. 'It was when his uncle thought I was Matthew's wife that I felt my world was all topsy-turvy' concluded Amanda.

'Oh darling, I'm so sorry about all this. I know we all enjoyed the concert but I thought you were on edge and it's no wonder. You were waiting to tell us about this.'

Hazel's voice was tremulous and Bruce looked at her with concern. 'We had no idea you had any sisters ...'

'That you were one of triplets' interrupted Hazel and, without pausing for breath, 'How could that woman do such a terrible thing?'

By now Hazel was trembling and Timothy stood up quickly. 'You've had a nasty shock. I'll make a pot of tea.'

'I didn't meet this person, who could be your aunt.' Hazel was grateful for the comfort of Bruce's hand on hers and continued, 'I only know she was elderly and felt she couldn't cope with a young child.' There was no need for Amanda to know that the name and address given to the vicar in the first place had been false, that she had been left on the vicarage doorstep and that the vicar's wife had cared for her while the necessary arrangements were made.

Amanda opened her mouth to protest that this wasn't true. Matthew had told her that Tessa and Jessica had a cousin, Keith who was five years older than them, but didn't want to cause her mother any further distress. Instead she said, 'You and Dad have been the most marvellous parents. Obviously I can't remember my natural parents but I'm sure they couldn't have been more loving and supportive.'

It was a few minutes later, after the tea had been poured and cups handed around that Hazel asked, 'What are you going to do?'

Amanda glanced at Timothy and then her parents. 'I don't want to upset anyone.'

'Do you want to meet Tessa?' enquired Bruce while Hazel said, 'Imagine yourself in her shoes. Tessa, who has just lost someone whom she loved dearly and thought was her twin, is excited when she learns that she could have a long-lost sister. I'm sure she would be very upset if you didn't attempt to meet her.'

Amanda nodded, nevertheless her expression was serious. 'Suppose we don't like each other?'

'I should think that's highly unlikely judging from Matthew's re-action' offered Timothy.

'If you don't meet her you'll never know' said Hazel and Bruce simultaneously when Amanda crossed the room to hug them. 'Thank you, you're both being very supportive about this. However I've only just returned, I'll have to wait until it's convenient.'

'In the meantime you could 'phone her' suggested Bruce.

'If Tessa shares her husband's enthusiasm she'll probably 'phone you' said Timothy.

'How could that woman separate triplets?' Hazel shook her dress before placing it on a hanger.

'You don't know for certain that they were triplets. That Amanda was one of them,' pointed out Bruce. 'At least they were too young to know anything about it.'

'That's true but even at that age everything changed for them. I must say Amanda was never any trouble.' Hazel removed cleansing cream, applied toner, then moisturiser and smoothed her eye-brows. 'However there is something I don't understand.'

'What's that?' Bruce was already in bed, reaching for a paperback.

21

'Why did the aunt behave like that, give the vicar in Bristol the wrong information so that she couldn't be traced? There's no harm in admitting that she and her husband couldn't afford to bring up three young children, in addition to their own son.'

'I couldn't answer that question at the time, and I still can't. However we do know that the aunt wasn't seen when she left Amanda on the doorstep, and that no one came forward when enquiries were made.'

'There might have been other relatives who would have gladly taken them, or even someone like us.'

'You couldn't have coped with three. Their natural parents probably had a large house and a nanny and, much as I love you, I couldn't have afforded that.'

Hazel nodded. 'I realise that but I can't forget the innumerable questions we were asked, not to mention the forms they gave us when we tried to adopt a child.'

'That was a long time ago.' Hazel laid her head on Bruce's shoulder as he held her close and reminded her that she had been very depressed at the time. 'You were so excited when our vicar came to tell us that he knew of a little girl who needed a home. A colleague of his, in Bristol, had 'phoned him about her that morning. I couldn't bear to think of you being disappointed again. We'd been let down twice when single mothers changed their minds, - decided to keep their babies.'

Hazel smiled drowsily. 'Amanda was so sweet and affectionate. She always liked a hug and a cuddle.'

'Even as she grew up.' Bruce kissed the top of Hazel's head. 'We were happy before but Amanda brought us closer, enriched our lives and I don't want to see you, or her, hurt through this chance encounter. Anyhow, that's enough for tonight. It's time we went to sleep.'

Meanwhile, in another part of Guernsey, in the bedroom of their small bungalow Amanda was carefully examining the contents of the top drawers of her dressing-table, muttering 'I know it's here, somewhere.'

'What are you looking for?' The first time Tim asked this question Amanda had been too engrossed in her task but now told him, 'My Birth Certificate' and then, 'Ah! here it is.'

'What's so important that you want to look at it now, at this time of night?' Once again the sight of Amanda's face glowing with excitement, a short white cotton nightie emphasising a slender figure and tanned limbs made Tim feel that he was an extremely lucky man and he urged, 'Come to bed.'

'Look at this.' Amanda got into bed, holding her Birth Certificate in two hands. 'Daughter of Irene and Richard Gilmour-Morgan. That could explain a lot of things.'

'What are you talking about?'

'I know I read this when Mum gave it to me on my eighteenth birthday but it's only just occurred to me who my natural parents were.'

'Can't this wait until the morning?' Tim stroked Amanda's shoulders and fingered the narrow straps.

'Don't you see, this could explain my interest and love of music, even at a young age.' Wide-eyed Amanda turned to gaze at Tim, 'Richard Gilmour-Morgan, my natural father, was a well-known concert pianist while Irene, my mother, was a singer. Neither Matthew or his uncle mentioned Tessa's maiden name but, if she is my sister, it'll be Gilmour-Morgan. Shall I 'phone and ask her?'

'Not at this time of night. Leave your Birth Certificate on the bedside table and turn off the light.'

Disappointed that there was no reply, that Tessa was not at home, Amanda decided to visit her mother when she finished at school that afternoon. Unaware of her tense expression Amanda was surprised when several of the older senior teachers enquired if she was unwell, or had problems with any of her pupils. Annoyed that she had allowed her distraction to become obvious she quickly assured them she was fine and that her pupils were all enthusiastic about a forthcoming concert.

'This is a lovely surprise' exclaimed Hazel, greeting Amanda with her usual smile and a hug. 'Have you time for a cup of tea?'

'Thanks,' then taking her Birth Certificate from her handbag Amanda said, 'Although I looked at this when you gave it to me, I hadn't realised until last night that my natural parents were Richard and Irene Gilmour-Morgan, that he was a well-known concert pianist and she was a singer.'

'Did someone tell you that at school today?'

'No. It was when I saw the name last night that I suddenly remembered one of the older teachers talking about concert pianists they had known when they were younger ..' and as Hazel started to say how sorry she was that they weren't interested in music at that time, Amanda shook her head and scolded, 'Don't you dare apologise. You were both marvellous when I wanted piano lessons, encouraged me over the years and it's thanks to you both that I got my present job.'

'Nonsense' and as Hazel pushed a mug of tea across the kitchen table, 'Your teacher always said you had a gift but, in view of what you've just told me, it's quite likely that you've inherited some of your talent from Richard.' Hazel gazed at Amanda over the rim of her mug, 'What's the surname on Tessa's Birth Certificate?'

'I don't know but I have been wondering about that all day. I was going to 'phone her last night but Tim said it was much too late, and I haven't been able to contact her today.'

'She's probably in her husband's antique shop.'

'You're fantastic! Why didn't I think of that? I'll 'phone her this evening but now I must dash.' Amanda kissed Hazel's cheek. 'Thanks for the tea.'

'Let me know if it's the same as yours' called Hazel as Amanda disappeared out of the back door and down the garden path.

CHAPTER FIVE

'Hello darling! This is a lovely surprise.' Matthew set down a Meissen figure of a Malabar musician on a Chippendale tea-table and moved towards Tessa, noting that for the first time since Jessica's death her cheeks were flushed and her eyes sparkling with excitement.

In the short time that it took for them to reach each other, moving carefully between a mahogany footstool and a Victorian davenport, Tessa extracted an envelope from her shoulder-bag and waved it in the air excitedly, 'Guess what this is?'

Regardless of any passers-by or would-be customers Matthew tilted Tessa's chin and kissed her. 'A letter from Amanda Lockwood?'

'No. It's from Susan Ratcliffe. She says she was our nanny' and aware of Matthew's puzzled expression, 'before our parents died. She read about Jessica's accident in The Evening Post and asks about Amanda.'

'Amanda?' repeated Matthew.

'Yes. Apparently there were three of us. We were triplets.' Tessa swallowed and rushed on, 'Don't you see. It's possible that Amanda in Guernsey really is my sister.'

'Hold on a minute, don't you think you're rushing it. How do you know this Susan is genuine?'

'She saw our wedding photograph in the paper' and ignoring Matthew's comment that a lot of people probably saw it, 'and also that of Jessica and Roger. Susan also says how sorry she was to leave and hoped that we were happy with Aunt Margaret and Uncle Laurence.'

'She could have heard about them from mutual friends.'

Tessa moved away from Matthew, picked up a Baccarat paperweight from a side table and placed this on the rosewood-top breakfast table. She then added a Paul Stankard paperweight and said, 'I expect the gentleman who bought the St. Louis paperweight will buy one of these Baccarat. They really are beautiful however, returning to Susan, why are you such a doubting Thomas? I'm sure she's genuine.'

'How can you know that? You were only a baby at the time' then, seeing Tessa's crestfallen expression Matthew gathered her in his arms. 'I'm sorry I'm being so unkind. I don't want you to be hurt.' Matthew gazed into Tessa's upturned face, annoyed that he had caused her threatening tears then, in a gentle voice, asked, 'Where does this Susan live? Did she tell you anything about herself?'

Tessa nodded and handed him the envelope. 'Yes, anyhow you can read this while I use your office to check my make-up.'

It only took a few moments for Matthew to learn that Susan lived in Shepton Mallet. Her husband and his brother, whose children she had looked after when she left Bristol, owned and ran a hotel there. Her own children were grown up and she was now a child minder for four children belonging to hotel staff. It all sounded plausible, thought Matthew and looking at Tessa, who had joined him again, kissed the tip of her nose and told her, 'You're beautiful and I love you.'

Tessa grinned, 'Is this the way to encourage prospective clients?' and glancing at the letter, 'What do you think?'

Matthew hesitated. He did not want to infer that Susan could be an impostor and reflected it was only natural that Tessa wanted to know more about the short period that Susan had been her nanny, and to see the photographs to which Susan referred. He knew that Tessa and Jessica had been upset that there were none of them as babies, that their questions about these had always been rebuffed and he had often wondered what had become of them. 'We'll talk about it this evening and perhaps, in the meantime, you can think of anyone who would remember her.'

'Some of the neighbours might but they've probably moved.'

'What about your cousin, Keith?'

'Him!' Tessa snorted in an unladylike manner. 'I didn't like him when we lived with Aunt Margaret and Uncle Laurence, and I still don't like him.'

'He's five years older than you so he might remember Susan.'

'I suppose it's possible.' Tessa looked thoughtful. 'Even when we were much younger Jessica and I always thought Keith was strange and we used to whisper about him. He always gave us the impression he was superior to us, that he knew something we didn't. And although he was very rude and unkind to his mother she was always buying him expensive presents. I don't think Uncle Laurence had a very happy life. We both felt sorry for him, he was the only person we loved....' Tessa stopped abruptly as a customer entered the shop.

As often happens, one customer attracts another and as Norman, Matthew's assistant, was having an early lunch break, Tessa was happy to talk about the various items in which they were interested. She was delighted when a tiny, rather wizened old lady bought a nine carat fancy link bracelet for her grand-daughter's eighteenth birthday, and again when a couple who had studied various items decided to buy the William and Mary gate-leg table with oval top for their new home. The husband, obviously an astute businessman, admitted he was impressed by Tessa's knowledge of so many items and told her that there was a vacancy for a senior sales person in his father's business in Bath and did not hide his disappointment when she explained that shop was her husband's, and she was therefore unable to accept his offer. To her amazement this did not deter him and he produced his business card telling her to 'phone him if she changed her mind.

As the door closed Matthew burst out laughing. 'You're marvellous! I was beginning to despair of both of those items, and you sold them without a qualm. We won't tell Norman, let him discover they've gone. He'll probably be green with envy at your success.'

Tessa giggled then the door opened again and a very tall white-haired gentleman with a stick entered and as Matthew moved towards him Tessa went back to the breakfast table. She had always been interested in antiques, loved reading about them thus widening her knowledge, and attending sales. She had met Matthew when viewing the contents of a large private house in Clevedon, and again the next day at the auction. She could still remember how nervous she felt but her employers had approved her report on the items in which they were interested, and Matthew's presence had given her confidence.

Tessa picked up and was studying one of the Baccarat paperweights when Matthew joined her, saying 'It's very pretty, isn't it?'

'Yes, they're all lovely however that gentleman wasn't here long. Did he buy anything?'

'An unusual cameo brooch. His wife had seen it and asked me to put it aside.' Matthew watched as Tessa, whose sapphire blue suit almost matched her eyes, moved towards the mahogany writing table, the red leather lined rectangular top making an ideal background for the items of antique jewellery which were displayed, and remembered the first time they met.

On Uncle Ben's instructions he had driven down to Clevedon to view the contents of a large house which were to be auctioned. Tessa was there, also viewing several items in which they were both interested. After exchanging names he had learnt that it was the first time her employer had sent her out to do this and she was apprehensive that, if he was satisfied with her report on these items, she might be sent to bid for them the following morning.

'Have you thought of anyone who might remember Susan?' asked Matthew that evening.

'Unfortunately no. I did think of the doctor but after we went to live with Aunt Margaret she took us to hers.'

'That's a pity.' Matthew noted Tessa's wistful expression and reached for her hand. 'Phone Susan and ask her to come and see you. Tomorrow if possible.'

'She'll be here about eleven o'clock. Can you come home for a while to meet her?' asked Tessa a few minutes later.

'That's no problem. Norman is quite capable of looking after the shop.' Looking at Tessa's sparkling eyes and glowing face Matthew hoped that this meeting would be a success. He did not want her to suffer any further disappointments.

'I wonder what she's like, if I'll remember anything about her' muttered Tessa the next morning as she plumped up the cushions on the settee, then immediately scolded herself. 'Don't be so stupid. I was only eighteen months old.' At that moment the doorbell rang, Tessa looked round the room again and glanced in the octagonal mirror, which had been a present from Uncle Ben, before opening the front door.

'Mrs. Ormerod?' The gray-haired woman standing on the garden path looked apprehensive and then, in a normal voice, 'Tessa?'

'Yes. You must be Susan, come in.'

Once indoors the two women just gazed at each other then Susan nodded, 'Oh, my dear, you're so like your lovely mother. How I wish she could see you now' and as Tessa stifled a sob, Susan hugged her murmuring, 'How I've longed to do this.'

It was some time later that Matthew stood in the doorway between the hall and the lounge observing Tessa and an attractive middle-aged woman as they gazed at each other with misty eyes, and holding hands. Then, as though she had sensed his presence Tessa glanced up, sprang to her feet and running towards him, pulled Matthew into the room. 'I'm sorry we're both rather tearful but it's rather emotional meeting someone who remembers my parents and is prepared to talk about them. Come and say hullo to Susan while I make some coffee.'

Susan stood up and held out her hand as Tessa left the room. 'I'm delighted to meet you, Mr. Ormerod, or may I call you Matthew?'

'Of course' and as Susan sat down again Matthew continued, 'Tessa has been so excited about your visit. She was absolutely devastated when Jessica died, - they were very close.'

'I'm sure they were but ....' Susan broke off as Tessa re-appeared carrying a tray. It wasn't until Susan had finished her coffee that she glanced at Matthew, who sat opposite, and then Tessa. 'I don't want to upset you but I would like to know what happened to your other sister, Amanda. As I told you in my letter, there were three of you.'

Susan spoke softly and was glad when Matthew moved to sit beside Tessa on the settee and put his arm around her. 'That's why your parents engaged me to look after you. Your mother, who was a lovely person, had kept remarkably well during her pregnancy, often said she could have coped with two babies with some help, but not three.' Aware that Tessa and Matthew were both bewildered Susan reached into her handbag, still talking. 'That's why I was so surprised, and very upset, when your aunt gave me notice. Said she wouldn't need me. I couldn't understand it. I knew she had your uncle and Keith to look after and that she didn't have any help in the house. I was puzzled as to how she would cope. However, you can see for yourself that there were three of you. Although it was rather hectic I took this when your parents brought you all home.'

Tessa gazed at the photograph, voice muffled. 'That's my parents?' Irene Gilmour-Morgan was holding a baby in each arm while Richard was holding the third.

'Surely you have the other photos of them and yourselves when you were babies?' But when there was no reply, 'Your mother had a copy of those.' Then, as Susan handed over more photographs, 'and these, which were taken at three monthly intervals. Your aunt must've taken them so you should have seen them.'

'She was always too busy or rebuffed us when we asked.' Tessa gazed at the photos and then looked at Susan. 'What happened to the other baby, Amanda?'

'I don't know my dear, that's why I asked you. You were all together and in good health when I left.'

'There was only Jessica and I when we went to school. I can't remember anything much before that, or aunt and uncle talking...'

'A young child can't disappear like that' interrupted Matthew and, as Susan's eyes widened, 'Your aunt must have made other arrangements for her.'

'Your grandparents, the Taylors, who lived in Scotland, wouldn't have taken just Amanda and I don't think they could have coped with all of you. Unfortunately neither of them enjoyed good health but I'm sure they wouldn't have wanted you to be split up.'

'Why didn't your aunt tell you that you had another sister, possibly when she told you about your parents accident?' asked Matthew.

Tessa ignored this question and asked one of her own. 'Could Amanda in Guernsey be our Amanda?'

It was Susan's turn to look puzzled and she echoed, 'Amanda in Guernsey?' then listened intently as Matthew spoke of his encounter in Exeter, 'Even my uncle mistook her for Tessa.'

Susan looked thoughtful. 'I suppose it's possible if she's the same age as Tessa and was adopted by a couple who lived in Bath.' Then, moving to the armchair vacated by Matthew and in order that she could look at him, Susan asked, 'Did this Amanda tell you any details about her adoption?'

'No, only that her parents told her when she was seven. However I'm sure she'll now be asking more questions.'

'How could you tell us apart?' asked Tessa, looking at the photographs again.

'At first, and even when I left, you each had a different coloured arm band but I had noticed and pointed out to your mother, the moles on your arms.'

'Moles!' echoed Tessa.

Susan then explained that Jessica had four little moles on her right forearm, Amanda's were on the left arm below the elbow, Tessa's were also on the left arm, above the elbow. These details had been added to the list of dates on which they had received their vaccinations.

Tessa turned to Matthew and holding out her left arm she studied this and said, 'Look, there they are. So I'm definitely Tessa.'

'Surely you didn't think you could have been Jessica.'

'No, but Aunt Margaret never spoke of any identifying marks such as moles and it never occurred to Jessica or I to annoy her by switching identities.' Tessa glanced at Susan, 'So Amanda should have four little moles just below her left elbow?'

'Yes' and transferring her gaze to Matthew, Susan asked, 'Do you intend to see her again?'

'We might go over for a weekend. Amanda is a music teacher so it might be difficult for her to get away during term.' Matthew was now standing and seeing that Susan was about to do the same, he continued, 'If you can spare the time, why don't you stay and have some lunch with Tessa. I'm sure there's all sorts of things she wants to know.'

CHAPTER SIX

'Why haven't I heard from Jessica's lawyer? It's a fortnight since the accident and a week since the funeral,' grumbled Keith Morgan with frustration as he banged his empty mug on the table. He had just returned from work and had a terrible afternoon.

Keith was a car salesman and had taken two potential clients out for a test drive but the first had not really been interested in buying a Rover, whilst the second hoped to part exchange his high-mileage uncared-for Volvo saloon. Keith had sworn under his breath as the Volvo owner drove off. He had really tried hard with both men, pointed out the pristine exterior, the comfortable leather seats, mahogany dashboard and later, during the drive, listened politely to their chat about houses, gardens and holidays. He had hoped that by selling just one car that afternoon he would achieve his target for the month, get an extra bonus from the manufacturer and possibly a free holiday.

'Why are you so certain Jessica has left you something?' asked Debbie.

'Tessa and her husband don't need it, and there's no one else.'

'Jessica may not have thought ....' and although Keith's eyes glittered angrily Debbie continued, 'She hasn't been here since I moved in, doesn't know how shabby the furniture is, or that the house is badly in need of redecoration.'

'It needs more than that. It's in a terrible state. I can't remember when my father spent any money on repairs, let alone anything else. Silly fool, - taking in Jessica and Tessa, even though they were my cousins. It probably kept him, or rather all of us, short. There must have been friends who could have taken them.'

'You always implied that your father had money.' Debbie's tone was accusing. 'I only saw the so-called lounge when I came here for the first time, it wasn't too bad then. I didn't see the other rooms until much later and I certainly didn't expect them to be so awful.'

'You could have re-decorated our bedroom.'

'Why me?' and when reminded that she was the one complaining Debbie suggested they could do it together. Then, before Keith could reply, she asked, 'Why didn't your father claim against the driver when your mother died?' Margaret Morgan had died three days after being knocked down on a pedestrian crossing. The driver had been traced, the registration number noted by a witness, and charged with reckless driving.

'I don't know. I tried to persuade him, even went to the police station to enquire what the procedure was, but he wouldn't listen to me.' Debbie had only known Keith for a year when the accident occurred but she remembered that Laurence had been too distressed to see anyone, even Tessa and Jessica. Then, all of a sudden Laurence, who was almost a teetotaller, started drinking heavily. Despite his lack of affection or respect for either of his parents, Keith had been shocked when his father suffered a massive stroke and died.

While Debbie made a list of essential repairs, although she had no knowledge when any of them would be carried out, Keith found himself thinking about his other cousin, - Tessa's and Jessica's sister, - wondering what had happened to her. He assumed she was alive, somewhere. If she had died as a baby he wouldn't have received so many expensive presents from his mother, - even when Tessa and Jessica moved out to share a flat. He could still picture his mother's face when she told him that he must never, never talk about the other baby . There had been many occasions when he had only to say 'I wonder ...' when she would glower at him warningly, then the next day there would be another present.

Glancing at Debbie's bent head Keith considered that he was lucky she had stayed with him so long. She had been on duty in Reception when he called for a prospective client and he had immediately noticed her stunning figure, friendly smile and that she was Head Receptionist. Debbie was not only very attractive, reflected Keith, she always cooked a good meal when she was off-duty in the evening and, in spite of its run-down condition, looked after the house. In addition she was good natured, always listening to his grumbles and hoping that she might re-consider her decision about the bedroom he said, 'Let's go out for a meal and have an early night.'

Debbie pushed the list aside and stood up, thinking they would probably end up by having a pizza in the wine bar round the corner, and that she would probably be expected to pay however, forcing herself to sound cheerful, she said, 'That sounds like a good idea.'

Ben Ormerod kissed Tessa on both cheeks then, holding her at arm's length, noted her sparkling eyes . 'How are you, my dear?'

'Very well, thank you.' Although she had only uttered a few words Tessa was almost breathless, the excitement of meeting Susan and the 'phone call from Amanda was still bubbling inside her.

Ben glanced from one to the other as, having ordered their aperitifs, he learnt of Susan's visit and saw the photos she had given Tessa. 'Susan and I didn't stop talking. She didn't leave until four o'clock. Then, just as we were ready to leave, we had a 'phone call from Guernsey' said Tessa.

Ben noticed that the head waiter was looking in their direction, 'Shall we study the menu or do you know what you would like to eat?' As regular diners at this particular restaurant Tessa and Matthew knew that the food was always superb and quickly chose their entree and main course, when Ben said 'I can see you're bursting to tell me about this 'phone call. How was Amanda?'

Tessa ignored this and said quickly, 'Amanda looked out her Birth Certificate on Thursday evening and tried to 'phone me several times yesterday. Although her mother gave her this on her eighteenth birthday the name of her natural parents didn't mean anything to her at that time. However, discovering that they were ..' Tessa paused and drank some of her dry martini and lemonade, aware that Ben was leaning forward with anticipation, 'Richard and Irene Gilmour-Morgan, she suddenly remembered one of the older teachers talking about concert pianists when his name was mentioned but, more important, she wanted to know the surname on my Birth Certificate.'

'So she really is your Amanda? Have you made any arrangements to meet her?'

It was with restraint that Tessa waited until they were seated at the table, the bread basket proffered and wine poured when she said, 'We're hoping to fly to Guernsey to meet Amanda next week-end but in the meantime, although I'm not very keen, we intend to see Keith. He was five years old at the time of the accident so he must have known there were three of us.'

'I'm surprised that Keith has never said anything.' Ben had met Keith at Tessa's and Jessica's weddings and considered him an objectionable young man while he thought that Debbie, his live-in partner, was attractive, smartly dressed and well-mannered. He had been very surprised that she had fallen for someone like Keith.

'I think Aunt Margaret bought his silence. We noticed that he was given expensive presents several times a year.'

38

At this Ben admitted that Keith had not created a very favourable impression and asked, 'Do you think he knows what happened? Even as a child he must have been curious.'

'Only he can answer that question but I doubt that Aunt Margaret told him in case he told us, hence the presents.'

'But why was it...' Matthew broke off as the plates were removed, 'such a secret?'

Tessa looked thoughtful. 'I don't know.'

Ben transferred his gaze to Matthew. 'I hope you're going with Tessa when she calls on Keith.'

'Of course. Like you I don't trust him and I certainly wouldn't want Tessa to be in that house without me.' Then, in reply to Ben's inquiry, Matthew told him that Roger was coming to lunch the next day, 'He was with a client so we only spoke for a few moments this morning.'

The topic of conversation then switched to antiques, Ben talking about the forthcoming sales of the contents of three large country houses, two situated in different areas of the Cotswolds and one near Stratford-on-Avon when both Tessa and Matthew expressed interest, the latter asking, 'Do you have a list of the contents?'

'Yes. I'll drop in a copy on Monday so you can study it. The houses are open for viewing two days before the sale. If there's anything listed that you're interested in I'll be quite happy to bid on your behalf or, if either of you would like to travel up with me, we could just take one car. Of course, you may prefer to make your own way there.'

'We'll look at the list and decide then' said Matthew.

'There are several comfortable hotels in that area, well-known for their cuisine, and I also have some very good friends I haven't seen for some time. I was thinking that I might decide to stay up there rather than come home and drive back. You could do the same.'

'I wouldn't want to cramp your style if you're meeting any of those attractive and wealthy widows you've mentioned on various occasions' teased Matthew. 'I'm quite content living on my own.' Ben picked up the dessert menu, 'shall we choose our sweet.'

'There's no need to ring the doorbell, just open the door, call out and walk in' Matthew told Roger as he ushered him into the lounge. 'Which would you prefer, a beer or something stronger?'

'Lager, please.' Roger smiled at Tessa as she crossed the room and kissed her on the cheek. 'Something smells good.'

'Roast lamb.' Tessa looked at Roger, glad to see him looking so well and wearing a pale blue short-sleeved shirt and pale gray trousers. She knew Olivia, his mother, ensured that if she wasn't cooking him an evening meal there was plenty of food in the 'fridge and that, in spite of his terrible loss, Roger was being sensible nevertheless she asked, 'How's Olivia?'

'Mum's fine. In fact, she's being quite fantastic. If I'm feeling low or in need of company she comes round, on the other hand she realises there are times when I prefer to be alone. However, what's all this about Amanda in Guernsey?' Roger knew about Matthew's encounter in Exeter and looking across at him, 'Tessa's a fine one. She invited me to lunch, told me she had received a 'phone call, that it was all rather exciting and then, that I would hear all about it today.'

'I'm sorry. We were going out and Matthew was urging me to hurry up.'

'That's right. Blame me' said Matthew.

'Refill your glasses and take them through to the dining-room' instructed Tessa.

'It's amazing that all this has happened now' said Roger after he had learnt about Amanda checking her Birth

Certificate. 'Jessica would have been so excited and I'm sure if she had known there were three of you, she would have insisted that Amanda should be found.' Then, looking at Tessa and Matthew, 'However it seems as though there's something strange about the whole situation. Why didn't your aunt or uncle tell you about Amanda? Or even Keith? He must have remembered that there were three of you.'

'He probably did and would have told us but we noticed that Aunt Margaret was frequently buying him expensive presents. Anyhow, we're going to see him tomorrow' said Tessa.

'We're both going. Although I don't know him very well I don't trust him' said Matthew.

'I only met him once, at our wedding, but neither do I. Nevertheless I did wonder what his girl friend, who's very attractive, saw in him. However, back to Amanda, is she coming to Bristol?'

'I don't think so but we're planning to fly to Guernsey next week-end.' In spite of talking they all finished their meal at the same time and as Tessa picked up the plates Roger told her, 'That was delicious.'

It was later, after they had eaten Bakewell tart and cream, the dishes had been loaded into the dishwasher and they were sat in the garden that Roger asked, 'Do you mind if I talk about the agency?'

'Of course not. We're both happy to listen and if we can help in any way, we'll be pleased to do so' said Matthew.

In the peacefulness of the shaded area of their garden Roger told them that Sarah Mortimer, whom he had taken out on several occasions before Jessica joined the agency, was constantly inquiring if she could do any cooking or household chores for him and he had resolved that, if she asked again, he would tell her that his mother had moved in. 'I don't like telling lies and I don't want her to leave' said Roger. 'Sarah's a good worker and that's important at the moment. This brings me to the crux of the situation, - Gregory. I just don't understand him, or his behaviour.'

'Is it still the same?' enquired Matthew who knew that Gregory was refusing to take any responsibility, accept any 'phone calls or even talk to Roger who had taken charge only four days after the accident.

'Yes. At the moment I've arranged for Rena to do some of the clerical work that I usually deal with, and the other girls are all very good but there are occasions when I need to be there which means that I can't be out with any potential clients.'

Matthew nodded. 'So, without meaning to be hurtful, you're minus two staff.'

'Exactly. Each time I ask Gregory if he can spare me a few minutes he just sits at his desk staring into space, grunts and tells me to get on with it. I've no idea how long he's going to be like this and the business certainly can't survive indefinitely.'

'Do you think he would talk to a doctor?' asked Tessa.

'I'm rather wary about suggesting it. Hopefully he might be better tomorrow but I'll let you know what happens.' Roger leant back in his chair, stretched out his legs and closed his eyes and, before Tessa and Matthew could reach for a Sunday paper, was sound asleep.

CHAPTER SEVEN

Keith's greeting was so curt, followed by 'I suppose you'd better come in,' that Tessa almost stumbled and was glad that Matthew was holding her arm.

As she stepped into the hall and followed Keith into the room overlooking the now untidy looking front garden and which Aunt Margaret had grandly called 'the lounge', Tessa wrinkled her nose in distaste. Debbie, clad in a scarlet track-suit, her shoulder length jet-black hair loose, was sprawled on the shabby settee and did not look up from the television programme she was watching, or even lower the sound. The surface of a long low coffee table was cluttered with two plates, one with the congealed remains of a half-eaten meal, cups, mugs and glasses.

'I suppose you're here to tell me the good news' said Keith as he stood by the window, his hands thrust into the pockets of his jeans emphasising their grubbiness and his paunch. 'I must say I'm surprised you've come. I thought it was usual to receive a letter from the solicitor.'

It was Keith's utterance of the last word that caught Debbie's attention when she reduced the sound while Tessa and Matthew exchanged glances but before either could speak Keith said, 'There's no need to look so dumbfounded. How much has Jessica left me?'

'I don't know and in any case why should she leave you anything?' queried Tessa.

'My parents worked hard to bring you both up. I ....'

'You didn't go short of anything' snapped Tessa. 'You had a good education and although you didn't excel in any of the sports in which you participated, you always made sure you had the best sports clothes and equipment. And as for your first remark, my father had arranged insurance to cover day-to-day needs and educational requirements. However, the reason for our visit is this.' Tessa held out a copy of the last photograph taken of Jessica, Amanda and herself. 'Why didn't your parents, or even you, - you were five years old at the time we came to live in your house, - tell us we had a sister?'

'Don't be so ridiculous!'

'What's this all about?' demanded Debbie and when there was no reply she got up and peered over Keith's shoulder. 'Ooh, aren't they sweet! Who are they?'

'They're just three ordinary babies who could belong to anyone' retorted Keith when Debbie's gaze travelled from him to Tessa and back again.

'That's nonsense and you know it' said Tessa. 'You and Aunt Margaret were regular visitors when we were tiny. In fact, you were fascinated that we all looked alike!'

Tessa watched as Debbie's expression became even more puzzled and, his face nearly scarlet, Keith began to bluster. 'You .. you don't know what you're talking about.'

'This photo, and others, we taken by our Nanny ...'

'Who's a cheat and a liar' burst out Keith.

'That's nonsense. She's a reliable, honest and caring person.' Matthew's gaze was unwavering and his voice icy. 'We know from other sources about your visits so why have you never spoken about the third baby?'

'She's dead' and when Tessa shook her head Debbie launched into Keith. 'That's a wicked thing to say, especially if it's not true.' And looking at Tessa, 'What's going on? What's this all about?'

'There were three of us. We were triplets. When my parents were killed as a result of a car crash Aunt Margaret took Jessica and I to live with them, but I'm sure you know all about this. However, we were never told that we had another sister, what happened to her, or where she was.'

'Oh my God, how terrible! But surely you missed her, wondered about her. Why didn't you ask your aunt?'

'Can you remember what happened when you were eighteen months old? Could you talk then?' and when Debbie shook her head Tessa turned to Keith, 'Didn't you ever wonder what had happened to her?'

'Why should I? She was just another cousin, same as you.'

Disgusted at Keith's lack of manners and the way he spoke Matthew moved closer to Tessa, ready to reprimand him and was surprised when she ignored Keith's last comment and asked, 'Why was Aunt Margaret so apologetic when she knew she wouldn't recover from her injuries? She kept asking us to forgive her.' And when there was no reply, 'Why did Uncle Laurence refuse to see us when he was so ill?'

'I don't know.'

'You probably do but for some reason you don't want to tell us.'

Debbie watched as Keith began to bluster. She was accustomed to his angry outbursts but she had never known him to be like this. At his insistence she had not visited either of Keith's parents in hospital, he had emphasised that they did not want any visitors but at the time she had doubted this.

Matthew's voice, now equally brusque, broke into her thoughts, 'Let's return to the photographs. Do you remember the three babies?'

'Oh all right, - yes, I do. But what's all the fuss about? Tessa and Jessica didn't remember their sister, so why should I enlighten them? My mother insisted that I shouldn't tell them.'

'Hence all the expensive presents. Perhaps she wanted to tell us just before she died but she didn't, did she? So why didn't you tell us afterwards?' persisted Tessa.

'I really don't know why you're making such a bloody fuss' muttered Keith.

'How can you say a thing like that?' exploded Debbie. 'You're a conceited selfish oaf with no feelings or thoughts for

45

anyone else but yourself.' Debbie turned to Tessa. 'I'm sure you'd have tried to trace her if you'd known about her.'

'Of course.' And looking directly at Keith, 'It's a pity you can't remember, however we won't waste any more of your time.'

Tessa and Matthew were out of the room before Keith could protest but to their surprise Debbie joined them as they reached the front door. 'I'm sorry about Keith's bad manners and that we weren't very hospitable. This has certainly been a shock but I'll let you know if he says anything that is relevant.'

Debbie watched Matthew unlock the silver-grey Volvo estate thinking that they were a really nice couple and that Keith was a fool. Tessa could easily oppose any legacy that Jessica might have left him.

At the same time, as they drove home, Tessa thought about Debbie. She had to admit that she didn't know much about her, only that she was Head Receptionist at the recently-restored hotel in the centre of Bristol. Tessa, who had not been back to the house in Redland since she and Jessica moved out, had been disgusted at both the outside and interior. It was obvious that no money had been spent on the property or replacing any of the furniture and she was surprised that Debbie was content to live in such a place.

Matthew's question about Keith's job brought Tessa back to the present when she said, 'He probably looks and acts like a different person when he's selling highly-priced cars. But as far as I'm concerned, he's still objectionable and I don't trust him.' Then, 'Keith was a mechanic before he became a salesman so he knows all about engines, perhaps he tampered with the brakes or some other part of Jessica's car? He knows where she lives and where she works. Do you think I should tell the Chief Inspector?'

'I'm sure he's found that out by now, and that he and Detective Sergeant Branch are considering all possibilities. I know one thing, I certainly don't want to go back to Keith's place again.'

Detective Chief Inspector Fowler sank into the comfortable armchair opposite Tessa and Matthew eyeing the coffee pot and plate of sandwiches with appreciation. It was five minutes later, having eaten several ham sandwiches and his coffee cup refilled that he asked, 'What's this new information that's suddenly come to light?'

Tessa and Matthew exchanged glances. Although they had agreed that Matthew would explain Susan's visit Tessa told the Inspector, 'Jessica and I have another sister. We were triplets.'

Jim Fowler's bushy eyebrows shot up in surprise and still holding a beef sandwich he listened as Matthew told him of Susan's letter and subsequent visit. 'You had no knowledge of her existence?' enquired Fowler as he studied some of the photographs Tessa had placed on the coffee table.

'No. We were only eighteen months old when our parents died and our aunt didn't tell us. Even now, although he admits to receiving expensive presents to ensure his silence, Keith is very reticent to concede to her existence.' Tessa glanced at Matthew who nodded, 'It's strange that I should have heard from Susan so soon after Matthew's exciting encounter in Exeter. Even Uncle Ben, who was staying there overnight, was confused.'

Fowler looked from one to the other, Ben had not told him of anything unusual occurring when they lunched together and he now asked, 'Is this something I should know?'

'There's no way it can be connected with Jessica's accident however, at the time it was quite a shock.' Although it was irrelevant the Inspector listened to Matthew's account of his meeting with Amanda Lockwood, Ben's re-action on seeing her and their evening together. 'It was quite amazing and whilst I knew it was impossible, almost like spending an evening with Jessica' concluded Matthew.

'Despite the resemblance to Jessica and Tessa, and her adoption, it could still be a coincidence, and certainly has nothing to do with Jessica's accident.'

'Amanda is definitely our sister,' and aware of the Chief Inspector's startled expression, Tessa continued, 'Amanda hadn't really looked at her Birth Certificate when it was given to her but she did so last Thursday and 'phoned me Saturday evening. The name of her mother and father is the same as ours, Irene and Richard Gilmour-Morgan.'

Fowler held a photograph in each hand and his gaze travelled from that of the Gilmour-Morgans and the three babies to that of the triplets taken on their first birthday. 'The likeness is incredible. How did your parents and nanny tell you apart?'

'By different coloured armbands and then Susan discovered we each had four moles in different places on our arms.' Tessa held out her arm indicating hers. 'I'm sure Amanda will be interested when I tell her about it.'

'It's certainly a different way of identifying anyone however I'm sure you realise that, even by establishing that Amanda Lockwood is your sister, this won't make any difference to our enquiries.'

Tessa nodded, her expression serious. 'It wasn't an ordinary accident, was it?' Tessa's voice faded and Matthew reached for her and squeezed her hand.

Fowler sighed. 'We're still making enquiries about anyone who had access to her car the previous day.' Jessica's car had been taken to a local garage where a police Accident Investigator had carried out an inspection. As a result of the engineer's report and the faults that were discovered, the car had been taken to the Forensic Science Service Laboratory in Chepstow in Gwent and he was now awaiting a report from a

Mechanical Scientist. Based on that report and that from the engineer, they would then have some evidence as to whether or not any mechanical parts had been tampered with.

The route usually used from the Bostock's home at Henleaze to the agency had been checked, and also that from the agency to the property at Chew Valley Lake when the police driver commented that Jessica had probably taken the steep slope too fast and braked too hard. The car had hit the barrier on the right hand side at speed and a sharp angle, the momentum causing it to somersault the barrier and crash down the hillside. The driver's further comment that an expert would have re-acted with the skilful use of gears and handbrake had also been noted.

'It's a pity there aren't any windows facing on to the parking area behind the agency' said Matthew.

'Even if there were, the staff might have been too engrossed in their work to notice anyone attempting to get into Jessica's or any other car.' Fowler stood up as he spoke, 'I realise it's of little consolation at the present time, but we will find the perpetrator. In the meantime thank you for your hospitality, Mrs. Ormerod. I will be in touch immediately there is anything new to report.'

CHAPTER EIGHT

Heather Wingate gave a sigh of relief as the 737 began its descent into Heathrow. Although they had spent five days in Penang after leaving Jakavata and had travelled first class, it had been a long overnight flight from Kuala Lumpur.

Closing her eyes Heather relaxed, remembering Arthur's excitement on his return from New York following a successful interview at the headquarters of the United Nations Organisation when he had accepted a post as an assistant resident representative at the United Nations Development Program Office in Santiago, Chile.

They had been married for five years during which time Arthur worked in a bank while she had been a secretary, however, during the last eighteen months Arthur had become more unsettled and finally decided that he didn't want to continue in banking. He had often spoken about an alternative career in another country.

On his return she learnt that, in addition to general clerical work, Arthur would be assisting independent experts from different UN agencies in their contacts with various government ministries on their travels around the country. He would also be responsible for the international general service and local staff working in the UNDP office.

Heather smiled, recalling her excitement when the triplets were born, seeing them for the first time, visiting Irene twice a week and marvelling at the three baby girls. They were just six weeks old when Arthur flew out to Chile and she had joined him two months later, attending the christening and becoming godmother to Jessica on the Sunday before her departure.

With help from the wives of UN international staff, British Council and Embassy staff she had quickly settled in

Santiago, and soon made the two-bedroomed flat more comfortable.

The first nine years of Arthur's UN career were spent in South America. After three years in Chile they spent two years in Bolivia and nearly four in Argentina. In all these countries he had found his knowledge of Spanish extremely useful, especially when local officials did not know of his fluency in their language.

The four years at the UNDP head office in New York were hectic then Arthur had itchy feet again and requested a transfer to the "field", in any part of the world. His request was granted and he was posted to Nepal, as Deputy Resident Representative at the UNDP office in Katmandu. From the luxury and comfort of New York this was quite a dramatic as, despite great changes over recent years, Nepal remained one of the least developed of the developing countries.

It was with some regret that after nearly four years Arthur took up a new appointment at the UNDP Regional office. This, however, was a good opportunity for him to expand and develop his knowledge and expertise on the UN's work in the Asian region, one with a multitude of cultures and problems.

They were on home leave in England when Arthur received an urgent call to return to Bangkok, prior to travelling to Jakavata, to become the Resident Representative for Indonesia. Although ambitious Arthur was saddened that this promotion was due to the tragic deaths of the Resident Representative and his deputy whom he had known well. The two men were en route to a meeting with Government officials in the distant province of Irian Jaya when their 'plane crashed.

Their years in Indonesia, where Arthur was, in all but name, UN Ambassador passed all too quickly and soon after reaching the age of fifty-seven, Arthur decided on early retirement.

Heather smiled, remembering the many friends she had made over the years. Her thoughts then turned to her voluntary work in a children's clinic in a poor district of Santiago, and her involvement with non-nursing work at the large mission hospital in Katmandu, where there were always injured and sick tourists.

It was half an hour later, seated in a chauffeur driven car heading for London that Arthur reached for Heather's hand. 'We're home, my darling and I'm sure, like me, you're delighted to be back in England. You'll now be able to meet Tessa.'

'It's ridiculous to think she's twenty-six and I haven't seen her, in fact any of them, since the christening, all due to Margaret's animosity.' Heather lapsed into silence, remembering the day she received the cable from Richard's solicitor, informing her of the accident. This had been followed by an airmail letter which contained a detailed account of the sad news. She had been devastated to learn of the deaths of her good friends, Irene and Richard Gilmour-Morgan, and also Felicity Deane.

They had been in Santiago at the time and although Arthur suggested she fly home Heather insisted this was not necessary, Laurence (Richard's brother) and his wife Margaret also lived in Bristol, and Susan, the nanny, was very capable. Unfortunately, over the years, there had been many occasions when Heather wished she had done so.

She had written to Margaret and when there was no reply, to Irene's parents, the Taylors, whom she had met at the christening. It was from them that Heather learnt that Margaret and Laurence had the children but that Margaret was always very abrupt and rude whenever they 'phoned, ignored their letters and did not even acknowledge the gifts they sent for the children. Although loathe to write to Laurence at the bank they had done so. He had replied immediately, apologised for Margaret's rudeness and assured them that the children were well.

Heather had therefore communicated with Laurence at the bank and, although she preferred to send presents, asked that accounts should be opened in each of the children's names, so that she could arrange for money to be paid into these, at Christmas and on their birthdays. She had been pleased to learn that the Taylors were going to make similar arrangements.

Unfortunately, in spite of her many requests for photographs none were forthcoming and, on the rare occasion that he did write, Laurence told her that the girls were all well. There was never any mention of their progress at school, their interests or how they spent the school holidays.

Over the years Heather became more disappointed that her suggestion that she should visit the children whenever she came to England was always rejected and she attributed this to Margaret's attitude. Nevertheless, it was whilst they were in New York that she suggested to Arthur that, providing Margaret and Laurence were agreeable, Amanda, Jessica and Tessa should come out during the Easter holiday. Arthur warned her that Margaret would probably reject this suggestion and even ignore her letter. The latter happened and once again she had been disappointed that Margaret was such a killjoy.

Although she had never met Jessica the news of her death was a terrible shock and Heather had been glad that they would soon be returning to England. Mr. Harcourt, the solicitor, also advised her that the police were investigating the crash and told her that if there were any developments before her departure date, he would inform her.

Unconsciously Heather moved closer to Arthur, regretting that she had not been there at the time to comfort Tessa and Amanda and, as though reading her thoughts, Arthur tightened his grip on her hand. 'I know you've written to the girls but it'll be easier to explain who you are when you actually meet them. I'm sure they're very curious about 'Aunt Heather' who was responsible for the substantial bank balances.'

'I felt that, at eighteen, they needed some independence from Margaret Morgan.'

'That was a good idea, especially as, according to Laurence, they wouldn't receive their legacies from the Taylors until they were twenty one.'

'And now they're twenty six.'

'Stop worrying and tell me which you would prefer to see while we're still in London, - a musical, straight play or ballet?'

'A musical, please. We both enjoy them.' Heather's eyes widened with enthusiasm. 'I'm sure the concierge at the hotel will be able to book seats for us. Do you have a preference?'

'No. I'll be happy with whatever you chose.'

CHAPTER NINE

Detective Chief Inspector Fowler felt his spirits lift as Detective Sergeant Branch greeted him with his usual smile. 'Message for you, sir. Can you spare a few minutes to see Inspector Knott in connection with the Bostock case?'

'I hope she's not likely to waste my time.'

'I doubt it. I've heard that in addition to being extremely attractive she's also a very efficient officer.'

'Right, let's hear what she has to say.'

Inspector Fowler accepted Isobel Knott's apologies that she had only learnt about Jessica's death the previous evening, when she returned from holiday, at the same time approving her slim uniformed figure, thick wavy blonde hair and golden brown eyes. 'Unfortunately I can't help you with information about possible suspects or motives but I can tell you about the triplet's early background, when their parents died.'

'That's more than twenty years ago.'

'I know. I accompanied the sergeant who informed Laurence Morgan about his brother's death and, although it's irrelevant, I shall never forget his wife's callous re-action. We then took Mr. Morgan to his brother's home when the Nanny was as devastated as Laurence. I can still picture those three little girls. They all looked exactly the same. Rosy-cheeked, reddish hair and absolutely adorable. While Susan (the Nanny) asked Laurence about the children's future, she was very concerned about Jessica, Tessa and Amanda, I sat on the floor and they played with the shiny buttons on my uniform. When I eventually left the house I couldn't help wondering who would care for them.'

'Margaret and Laurence Morgan brought up Jessica and Tessa' offered Fowler.

'But what about Amanda?' and ignoring Fowler's comment that she had a good memory Isobel told him, 'I read about Margaret Morgan being the victim of a hit and run, and not long after the announcement of Laurence's death. I also saw Tessa's and Jessica's wedding photographs in The Evening Post and waited for Amanda's but, until now - nothing. Then, on my return from holiday I learnt about Jessica's accident.' Isobel leant forward. 'I've only read what was reported in the paper but was it an accident?'

'No. We suspected that the brakes had been tampered with and after it had been inspected by an Accident Investigator the car was taken to the Local Science Service Laboratory at Chepstow. We're now awaiting the engineer's report.'

'Who, or why would anyone cause Jessica's death?' And in the same breath, 'Although Tessa is married and has a cousin, Keith, she must be devastated.'

Jim Fowler nodded. 'Fortunately her husband, Matthew Ormerod, is very supportive but I get the impression that Tessa doesn't particularly like Keith. I must say I considered him rather unpleasant, when questioned.'

'He must have inherited that from his mother. However, whilst I appreciate that you're busy, do you know what happened to the other triplet, Amanda?'

Fowler suppressed a sigh and quickly recounted all that he knew, concluding, 'I think Tessa and her husband will be going over to Guernsey to meet Amanda.'

'Thank you. I must say I'm not surprised at Margaret Morgan acting like that, she really was an unpleasant woman.' Isobel stood up but before moving she looked directly at the Chief Inspector, 'Would it be possible for me to meet Tessa? As I said earlier I've often wondered what happened to those three little girls and I'd like to tell her, when I'm off-duty, how much I enjoyed that short time with them.'

Fowler sighed. 'I suggest you 'phone beforehand, and I'm sure I can rely on your discretion. She'll probably be pleased to meet someone who remembers her at that age.'

As the door closed Fowler looked across at Sergeant Branch, 'I wouldn't mind having Knott on my team. She's an intelligent and attractive woman who's done very well.'

Branch nodded, reflecting that it was unusual for his boss to voice his opinion of any female officers and silently agreed with Fowler's final remark. 'That was very interesting but I doubt that it has any relevance to Jessica's death.'

When Detective Sergeant Ivan Branch learnt that Jessica Bostock was the daughter of Richard and Irene Gilmour-Morgan he immediately remembered that his mother had been a great admirer of the concert pianist. Although in her eighties Mrs. Branch had been delighted to talk about the pianist when Ivan visited her on the following Sunday and recalled the concerts she had attended. Aware of his mother's excellent memory he had been startled when she also said that the Gilmour-Morgans had been the proud parents of triplets. Within minutes an old magazine containing photographs of the pianist, his wife and the triplets was produced when Mrs. Branch concluded, 'Although Irene had an excellent nanny she gave up her career, which was a great pity - she had a marvellous voice. Some reports said she would return when the children were older. Not only did the three little girls lose their parents, the general public lost two gifted artists. I wonder if any of the girls have inherited their parents' musicality?'

Recalling his mother's conversation Branch started when Fowler's voice cut through his thoughts, 'The 'phone call prior to Knott's arrival was from Matthew Ormerod. Keith told him that the third baby was called Amanda but he doesn't know what happened to her. His mother only brought two of the babies home and I learnt from Tessa last night that

Margaret Morgan was constantly buying him expensive presents so he must have known something. Tessa and Jessica couldn't possibly know, even remember. They were only eighteen months old.'

'I wonder if, although he was only five at the time, Margaret Morgan told Keith that Amanda had been adopted but warned him not to tell anyone, and that might account for the presents?' Branch paused but only for a moment, 'Why didn't Margaret tell Jessica and Tessa when they were older? Give them a chance to trace their sister, or even do so herself?'

'That's something we'll never know. However, returning to Jessica's accident and her car, it's a pity there aren't any windows overlooking the parking area. Although Gregory Niven, Roger and the other staff at the agency have been questioned I think you should see them again.'

Branch nodded and Fowler continued, 'The two main beneficiaries are Roger and Tessa. In both cases their alibis have been substantiated, - Roger didn't leave the agency all the afternoon while Tessa was in the antique shop. Norman, their assistant, had lost his voice.'

'As far as motive is concerned Roger, who wasn't short of cash beforehand, is going to do very nicely and, to our knowledge, there isn't another woman. Tessa doesn't need her legacy either.' Fowler had noticed that for the last few minutes Branch had been fidgeting and aware that the sergeant preferred to be active told him, 'See what you can find out about Niven. And Keith Morgan. Perhaps his girl friend, Debbie Ashe, can help you.'

'It was all very interesting and informative however I think you'll want to see Niven and Morgan yourself' commented Sergeant Branch when he returned that afternoon.

'Come in, sit down and start at the beginning.' Fowler leant back in his chair and wriggled to make himself more comfortable.

'I saw Keith Morgan first. I must say he looked the part: smart suit, white shirt, striped tie and polished shoes.' Branch produced his notebook and continued. 'He repeated his previous statement, - that he had taken a potential buyer on a test drive that afternoon. Keith then added and the following is an omission for which he apologised, that he took the client home and, on his way back to the sales room he was held up at the traffic lights near the agency. Whilst there he noticed Gregory come out and hurry round the corner to their parking area, which was also in sight.' Branch paused, picked up the cup of tea which had been brought in soon after his return and resumed, 'Keith then thought that, if there was sufficient space for the Rover, this would be a good opportunity to call in and see Jessica however, as he parked Gregory was just lowering the bonnet of a car which Keith recognised as Jessica's. Keith introduced himself, learnt that it was not convenient to see Jessica and ....'

Branch stopped abruptly and swallowed the remainder of his tea as Fowler growled, 'Stop prevaricating and come to the point. What did Niven say?'

'He wasn't very happy. Grumbled about staff ineff...'

'I'm not bothered about that' interrupted Fowler tersely, 'but I would like to know what Gregory was doing to Jessica's car.'

'He denied touching it. He said that he had gone out to fetch the details of a property from his car. He also stated that Keith was seated in the Rover when he left the parking area however, on reaching the corner he glanced back and saw that Keith was standing by Jessica's car. He assumed Keith was leaving a message on the windscreen and thought no more about it.'

'H'mph!' grunted Fowler. 'So they both had an opportunity to tamper with the brakes. Moving on, what did Keith's girl friend have to say?'

'Debbie was very co-operative.' Branch had noticed the dark shadows under her eyes and the slowly-fading bruises on her arms but this was not the moment to comment on those. 'She repeated that she was on the 3 - 10p.m. shift that Friday afternoon and, although she holds a driving licence, she had never driven Keith's car and knows nothing about brakes.'

'Did she know anything about Keith trying to see Jessica on the Friday afternoon?'

'No, but she did volunteer the information that he had 'phoned Jessica the previous evening. Apparently he asked her for a loan so that he could arrange for essential repairs to be carried out on the house. Jessica refused and Keith was furious.'

'When he probably took it out on Debbie' and seeing Branch's surprised expression Fowler nodded, 'Yes, I did notice her bruises on our first visit. However, returning to Keith, why did he want to see Jessica on that Friday afternoon?'

'He didn't say and at the time I didn't know about his 'phone call the previous evening. Perhaps he hoped Jessica would change her mind.' Then, in reply to Fowler's next query, 'Debbie only heard part of the conversation.'

'But Roger probably heard Jessica's side of it. It was a pity you couldn't see him this afternoon however find out if he's home yet and, if so, tell him we're on our way.'

Ten minutes later and silently cursing the indecisive driver in front of him Branch asked, 'Do you think the refusal of a loan would provide Keith with a motive?'

'It's possible. We know his temper is easily roused and that he can be violent but it really depends on how much he wanted.'

'Why did that sergeant question Gregory and not us?' Sarah Mortimer, one of the property negotiators, looked at Rena Lessiter, Gregory's secretary.

'I've no idea. He didn't refer to the detective's visit when I took his post in for signature. In fact, he didn't speak at all. He looked as though he was in a trance.'

'What's the matter with him?' Lisa Edwards and her colleagues from the agency occupied their usual corner table in the wine bar on the other side of the street.

'He certainly doesn't look as smart as usual.' Sarah sipped her wine. 'Only a few weeks ago he was telling us all to improve our appearance.'

'That was before Jessica's accident' offered Rena.

'Gregory is certainly very upset about that. In fact he seems to be more cut up than Roger and ...

Lisa cut short Sarah's comment that Roger was dealing with most of Gregory's administrative work as well as his own, 'We all know that Gregory was upset when Jessica and Roger announced their engagement but he seemed all right at their wedding.'

'Didn't Jessica look lovely that day? And to think it was only two years ago. Poor Roger.' Sarah sighed and then noticed Rena's expression. 'Why are you looking like that?'

'I was just thinking about the Friday afternoon before the accident, when Gregory told Roger to go out to the property at Chew Valley Lake instead of Jessica.'

'But he didn't, Jessica went as arranged. Do you know why?'

'Roger could see that Jessica was disappointed at this sudden change and suggested she should go, as previously arranged ....' Rena's voice faded. She had just remembered that earlier that Friday afternoon, whilst dictating the specifications of a bungalow at Portishead, Gregory had stopped suddenly, saying he couldn't remember all the details which were in his car, and had rushed out to fetch them. However, when he returned he didn't refer to them or why he was empty-handed. In fact, his hands were oily and he had told her to carry on with the other letters he had dictated.

Unaware that Sarah and Lisa had been nudging each other and whispering Rena was startled when Sarah asked, 'Is there something we should know?'

'What .. what do you mean?'

'Why did you stop so suddenly?

'Were you thinking of the afternoon Gregory came in with oily hands?' This came from Lisa and when Rena nodded, 'It was the afternoon before Jessica's accident. Is that why you're looking so worried?'

Rena hesitated for a moment. 'He went to fetch some papers from his car but came back empty-handed. He didn't even refer to the property specification he'd been dictating.'

'Would either of you like another drink?' enquired Sarah but Rena and Lisa both shook their heads.

During the next ten minutes Lisa's suggestion that Gregory could have been repairing a minor fault to his car was quickly veto-ed when she pointed out that, if Roger had driven out to the Chew Valley property he would have been the victim instead of Jessica, and shouldn't the police be informed?

'No' said Rena adamantly. 'There's such a thing as loyalty and we've all worked for Gregory since he started the agency.' Then, seeing their expressions she explained, 'If the police hear about Gregory's oily hands and new instructions they'll immediately suspect him and, sooner or later, find a motive.'

'That might not be so difficult' offered Sarah. 'If he's still in love with Jessica he could have been jealous of Roger. Wanted him out of the way.'

'That's another ridiculous suggestion. We don't say anything to the police.'

Lisa and Sarah exchanged glances and it was the former who said 'Let's wait until the weekend. Perhaps an arrest will have been made by then.'

'Do you know who did it? Tampered with the brakes, caused Jessica's death?' and before either detective could reply Roger continued, 'When I heard you'd called at the agency this afternoon I thought you'd arrested someone.'

'Not yet, unfortunately.' Detective Inspector Fowler chose a straight-backed winged armchair and looking directly at Roger who was still standing in the doorway, asked, 'Do you remember your wife receiving a 'phone call from Keith on the Thursday evening?'

'Yes. He had the audacity to ask for a loan, - £5,000. Wanted to get the decorators in. Jessica was furious. We've only seen the house from the outside and that looks awful, so I dread to think what the inside looks like. However she suggested he carry out the necessary repairs and any redecorating himself. His reply was vulgar and definitely threatening.' Roger paused, his gaze travelling from Branch to Fowler when he suddenly exclaimed, 'It must have been Keith! He's always worked with cars, did his time as an apprentice mechanic and is now a salesman. Why didn't I think of it before, where was he that afternoon?'

'In spite of everything Roger's always been pleasant and polite however that's the first time I've seen him so het up.' Fowler slid into the passenger seat, at the same time considering what was known about Roger. He was liked by the staff at the agency and regarded as reliable and a hard worker by Gregory Niven. He had been popular with the staff at his previous job and his employer had regarded him as dependable and hardworking.

'With good reason, if Keith is our man. We now know he had the knowledge, opportunity and motive but we need a witness.' Branch glanced at Fowler, 'Are you going to repeat the appeal? Although a side road it's a busy thoroughfare for pedestrians and motorists. It's possible someone saw Keith there.'

Fowler turned his head to gaze across the Downs and beyond to Leigh Woods. 'Yes. This case is dragging on and the Chief Superintendent isn't very happy, so the sooner an arrest is made, the better.'

CHAPTER TEN

'Who is it?' asked Matthew as Tessa's eyes widened and she whispered, 'Who are you? What do you want?' then, as Matthew joined her on the settee and in a normal voice Tessa continued, 'I'll probably be included in the next series but I don't know when it starts.'

Matthew inclined his head, hoping to hear the caller's voice then Tessa was talking again. 'As I told you before, we don't know the owners' addresses but in any case I wouldn't tell you.' There was another pause then, 'The idea of considerable wealth doesn't appeal to me and I can't tell you what I don't know.'

The next instant Matthew put one arm around Tessa while, with his free hand he pressed 1471 and, when there was no response, swore. 'Damn! He must have been in a public call box or using a mobile phone.' Then, worried by the sight of Tessa's pallor, quivering lips and trembling body he asked. . 'Are you all right?'

Tessa smiled wanly. 'I'll be fine. It was the shock of hearing that voice .... but I would like a drink.'

Matthew watched Tessa drink this, annoyed that he had been unable to trace the caller.

'Are you sure it was the same man who approached you after the antique programme?'

Although it was late and had been another busy day Detective Inspector Fowler had arrived ten minutes after Matthew's call.

Tessa nodded. 'Although that was last autumn I'm convinced it's the same person. It was the impediment in his speech that I recognised.'

Two years had elapsed since Tessa, due to the death of a well-known personality on the Antique Roadshow team and her specialised knowledge of the same items, mainly paper weights and snuff boxes, had been asked to join the panel. At first she had been apprehensive about accepting but Matthew and Ben had urged her to accept. Before long she found the other members of the team helpful and friendly, enjoyed meeting the owners of, on occasions, very valuable antiques and the interest shown by the spectators.

It was the previous autumn that the burglaries from the homes of the antique owners began. Disappointed that, in spite of advice and encouragement from the police, these owners had not photographed the very expensive items which were stolen, Inspector Fowler arranged that a team of plain-clothed detectives, including officers who specialised in dealing with the theft and recovery of antiques, should travel to different parts of the country where these programmes were being made, in order to mix with the owners, spectators and experts.

At first it was established that only easily transportable and saleable antiques were stolen but when really valuable items began to disappear Fowler, keenly aware that there was no reference or description of these in their specialised computer system, turned to his old friend, Ben Ormerod. At their second meeting Matthew, whose presence had been requested by Ben, suggested that there were probably some wealthy collectors who might be behind these later robberies. These people were often prepared to pay ridiculous prices for certain pieces which would then be kept behind 'locked doors'.

When Jessica's accident occurred Fowler had wondered if she could have been mistaken for Tessa, recalling the occasion when Tessa had been observed talking to a man whom one of the officers had regarded with suspicion for some time. It had been noted as a very brief conversation, the man had obviously questioned her because Tessa shook her head angrily and quickly walked away. This had occurred immediately after her conversation with the owner of the snuff boxes which she had just valued. When questioned Tessa stated that the man had wanted to know the owner's address which she had naturally refused to give him.

Owners, some drove many miles, in some cases from neighbouring counties, were always advised not to reveal their addresses on these programmes. Although aware of the police presence, that the televion team were also extra vigilant, Matthew and Uncle Ben, who were concerned for Tessa's safety, suggested that she be replaced by another expert but this idea was rejected by Fowler. However, owners were advised to return home in a round-about route and, if possible, take note of any cars or other vehicles following them. Advice that very expensive articles should be photographed and thus put into the specialised computer system was repeated.

'Is .. ' Tessa hesitated. 'Is there any way this man could be involved with Jessica's accident. Could .. could he have mistaken her for me?'

'Nonsense!' said Matthew tightening his grip on Tessa's hand at the same time flashing Fowler a warning glance.

'Highly unlikely. These robberies started last autumn as you know' said Fowler, thinking it was unfortunate that Matthew had been unable to trace the call, and making a mental note to check the photographs taken during the making of that particular programme.

Fortified by a canteen breakfast of bacon, eggs, tomatoes and fried bread, followed by two slices of toast, Detective Inspector Fowler told Inspector Kershaw, who was in charge of the antique robbery investigations, to apply for an authority through the Assistant Chief Constable for a tape recorder to be placed on the Ormerod's 'phone at home. This way any conversation between Tessa and the man with the speech impediment could be properly recorded. He also asked Kershaw to look out the photographs taken on the day that Tessa had been approached.

Five minutes later Kershaw placed a file on Fowler's desk. 'I've picked out the six shots of Tessa Ormerod, sir. Would you like me to 'phone her?'

'No, but you can see her when she comes in.'

Fowler knew that Tessa was annoyed that their privacy was to be invaded but anxious that her position on the team should not be jeopardised, had agreed to study the photographs that had been taken. Fowler was also aware that, up to that morning, none of the other experts had been approached or received any intimidating 'phone calls and now wondered if it was because she was the youngest, most attractive and possibly gullible, that Tessa had been chosen as the victim. Although the producers had at first disagreed, the other experts had been advised of the latest development, and thus warned to be on their guard.

'These are the photographs taken last autumn.' Detective Inspector Kershaw indicated the photographs spread out on the table, 'I hope you can remember what he looked like' and as Tessa sat down he added, 'Take your time.' Kershaw had seen Tessa on several occasions at different venues when the programme was being made, noted that she was an attractive young woman but now considered that, although pale and wearing a dark blue skirt and white blouse, she was absolutely stunning.

There were two shots of each person and Tessa quickly pushed those of a bald-headed man with protuberant eyes, aside. Her attention lingered on those remaining then another two were rejected. Kershaw did not watch Tessa, reading yet again what had been said to her the previous autumn and on the 'phone, but was aware that there was only one set left.

'That's him but he could look different now.'

Kershaw stood up and looking over her shoulder noted that she had chosen the slightly older man and commented that he and the one she had just rejected were the same height, medium build, thin featured and both wore a belted raincoat. The photographer had caught them full face and although Tessa looked very smart and attractive Kershaw concentrated on the man standing beside her. He had never doubted his powers of observation but gazed at Tessa with admiration when she said, 'I'm sure you realise he would look very different with grey hair and a moustache. And if he grew a beard, false ones unless properly applied aren't always safe, that would partially conceal his weak chin. He's obviously a vain person, look at the shape and apparent smoothness of his eyebrows so he might try to eliminate any lines. That would also alter his appearance.'

Kershaw nodded. 'How can you tell that his voice and that of the caller is the same?'

Tessa paused, smiled her thanks at the WPC who placed a cup of coffee on the table and looked across at Kershaw, who was now sitting. 'He's well-spoken, probably had a public school education, doesn't have an accent or any trace of a dialect but there was an impediment in his speech when he used certain words.'

'Such as?' prompted Kershaw and five minutes later, after Tessa had recounted both conversations, commented, 'You have a remarkable memory.'

'Although brief, it's not the sort of conversation you forget, especially his last remark, "I'm sure you could find out some addresses. I'll be in touch in case you change your mind and have some information for me."' Tessa glanced at the Inspector, 'I'm not the nervous type but, if and when he does 'phone, I hope you don't want me to ....'

'We only want you to keep him talking as long as possible' interrupted Kershaw.

'What if I see him in the street?'

'Go to the nearest 'phone and ring me or one of my team. Don't attempt to follow him. We've people trained to do that and deal with any unforeseen incidents.'

'He doesn't look the rough type but that doesn't mean he isn't.' Tessa looked thoughtful, 'His hands were well-kept and I noticed he had long slim fingers and manicured nails.'

CHAPTER ELEVEN

'It's incredible! So much is happening I can hardly believe it. Isobel Knott, who was a WPC at the time and accompanied Uncle Laurence when he came round to tell Susan the terrible news, is coming to see me this afternoon and to-morrow morning I'm going to meet Heather Wingate. I suppose I should call her Aunt Heather.'

'It's a pity we're going away for the weekend or you could have spent more time with her' said Matthew as he handed Heather's letter back to Tessa and then nodded when she pointed out that, as Heather's husband had retired, they might decide to live in England. 'That'll mean I can see her at any time. We can get to know each other.'

Eager to share Tessa's excitement but anxious to learn how she had fared at the police station Matthew had suggested they lunch together. They were now seated in a wine bar a few doors from his shop and Matthew seized the opportunity to ask, 'Did you pick out the photograph of the man who spoke to you?'

'Yes. There were only three taken on that occasion so it wasn't difficult.'

'What's the inspector in charge of that investigation like?'

'Re-assuring, efficient and probably in his mid-thirties. However, since hearing from Inspector Knott and receiving Heather's letter I haven't thought about last night's 'phone call.' Then, after a momentary pause, 'Heather must be a very kindhearted person.' Tessa remembered the letters she and Jessica had received on their eighteenth birthday. They had both been apprehensive about visiting Mr. Harcourt, their late parents' solicitor, and been amazed when he told them about the bank accounts that had been opened in their names, by Jessica's godmother, Heather Wingate. He had also explained that Arthur Wingate was now the U.N. Resident Representative in Indonesia and, in reply to their questions, told them that Heather and Arthur had spent some time in different countries in South America, New York, Nepal and Bangkok.

Tessa recalled that she and Jessica had been aghast to learn that, over the years, their Aunt Margaret had rejected Heather's request to visit them whenever she was in England. Aunt Margaret had become even more awkward and unpleasant ever since they left school the previous July and this knowledge had been the last straw.

Six weeks later they had moved into a small but adequate flat. Aunt Margaret had been furious, declaring they were ungrateful and incapable of looking after themselves while Laurence tried to dissuade them but this did not deter them. Although sparsely furnished they were on their own and, accompanied by one of her colleagues from work, which was a firm of valuers and auctioneers, Tessa attended auctions and gradually acquired the necessary items.

'I'm looking forward to meeting Heather and Arthur. They must have had a very interesting life, and he must be very clever.' Tessa ate the last mouthful of lasagne and dabbed her mouth with the serviette. 'I know Heather has suggested we have coffee at the hotel but I thought I would ask them home for a meal in the evening.'

'That's a good idea. It'll give me a chance to meet them both.'

'I'm sure you're curious as to why I wanted to see you so I won't waste any time.' Isobel Knott had greeted Tessa in a friendly manner, offered her condolences and now, seated opposite Tessa, resumed, 'As I told you on the 'phone, I was the WPC who accompanied your uncle when he called to tell your nanny the terrible news. You were all sat on the floor, looking absolutely adorable and were quite happy when I joined you there.'

'Fancy you remembering, - that was a long time ago.' Tessa was amazed that Isobel, who wore a smart emerald green trouser suit, was very tall, slim and had the flawless complexion of a fashion model, should be a police inspector.

'Yes, it was. I often thought about you all, in fact I've never forgotten that morning. At the time I thought Susan was a really lovely person. She was so concerned about you all. How long did she stay with you?'

'She didn't.'

Isobel's expression indicated her interest as Tessa recounted that Susan had been given notice, and that only she and Jessica were brought up by their Aunt Margaret and Uncle Laurence. 'However, after all these years, I met Susan last week. Over the years she had read of the deaths of our aunt and uncle, Jessica's and my wedding, and then Jessica's accident. It was the latter which prompted her to write to me and I was thrilled to see the photographs taken when we were first brought home, at our christening and those taken by her, when she came to see me.'

Isobel selected and studied some of the photographs which were on the low coffee table between them and, in reply to her enquiry, learnt that, without any warning, Susan had been told she was no longer required and therefore didn't know what had happened to Amanda.

Tessa then recounted Matthew's visit to Exeter the previous week, his encounter with someone whom, although he knew it was impossible, he thought was Jessica and whose name was Amanda. 'His Uncle Ben, who was also in Exeter, also mistook Amanda for me.' Tessa refilled their cups 'and during the evening which they spent with Amanda, they learnt that her parents had been living in Bath when they adopted her.'

Isobel's cup clattered against the saucer. 'Have you met her? Is she your sister?'

'The answer to your second question is that the surname on her Birth Certificate is the same as ours and, in reply to your first, we're flying to Guernsey on Friday and meeting them that evening.' Then, before Isobel could ask the obvious question Tessa explained that Amanda and her adoptive parents had lived in Guernsey since she was eleven, that Amanda was married and a music teacher.

'It's all so incredible, like finding the missing pieces in a jigsaw. I hope your enjoy your trip to Guernsey and, whilst I realise it's nothing to do with me, I would like to hear about it.'

'That's really kind of you. I'll 'phone you when we return.'

It was later that same afternoon that Amanda told her mother that Tessa and Matthew were arriving on Friday. 'They'll be staying at our favourite hotel in town and have invited us all for dinner on Friday.'

'What do you mean by all?' queried Hazel.

'They want to meet you and Dad.'

'That's very kind of ...' Hazel faltered but before she could continue Bruce spoke. 'You'd like us to be there, wouldn't you?'

'Please, Dad. I know Tim will be with me but I need you and Mum as well.'

'Of course we'll come.' Bruce reached for and squeezed Hazel's hand. 'We're as anxious as you to meet Tessa.'

'Why are you so late and what do you mean by telling the police how I spend my time?'

Debbie had scarcely closed the front door and stood with her back against it as Keith, his face flushed and eyes glittering angrily, swayed on his feet. 'We're short-staffed, a coach full of guests arrived late and I certainly haven't told anyone anything about you. In any case I don't know what you're doing at any specific time of the day.'

'Um ...' Keith slurped some of his whisky, started to back along the hall and stumbled.

Debbie was tired. It had been a hectic afternoon and evening but, anxious that Keith's temper didn't turn to violence, she followed him into the living room. Sinking into the nearest chair and wary of his reply she asked, 'What's happened?'

'There's a police appeal, it was made at the end of the regional news. They want to know if anyone was seen loitering, or acting suspiciously in the car park belonging to the estate agency on the Friday afternoon before Jessica's accident.'

Debbie nodded. 'That's understandable. But why are you so worried?'

"Cos I was there, as you and they know.'

'But I didn't know. You didn't tell me that you had seen Jessica.' Debbie waited for Keith to explode but this didn't happen.

'I didn't see her.' Keith drained his glass and quickly recounted his decision to call on Jessica and his encounter with Gregory when he learnt that Jessica was very busy. 'After Gregory went back to the office I sat in the Rover for a few minutes and then drove back to the sales room.'

'There's nothing suspicious about that.' Debbie covered her mouth as she yawned. 'Had Gregory just come back when you arrived?'

Keith shook his head as though to clear it when Debbie wondered if he was trying to remember something or if it was because he had drunk too much whisky. 'He ... he was standing by Jessica's car but I suppose it's possible. D'you want a drink? '

'No thanks. I'm too tired. All I want to do is sleep.'

Gregory looks worse today, thought Rena the following morning. She had been startled when he suddenly appeared in his office doorway and, before she could hang up her jacket, he said tersely, 'Come in. You won't need your note book.' His dark eyes emphasised his pale, almost gaunt features, his tie was awry, his suit creased, his shoes unpolished and to her astonishment he demanded, 'What did you tell the police about the Friday afternoon before Jessica's accident?'

'Nothing. It wasn't mentioned.'

'But surely when Detective Sergeant Branch was here on Tuesday ...'

'He didn't speak to me or anyone else' cut in Rena. 'He left as soon as he came out of your office. I was only questioned once.'

Gregory ran his fingers through his already dishevelled hair. 'Then why the police appeal?' and seeing Rena's puzzled expression he told her, 'It was on the radio and television last night and this morning. They want to know if anyone was seen loitering in our parking area.'

A picture of Gregory's oily hands flashed before her eyes but despite this Rena asked, 'How would I know anything about that? There's no windows facing the car park.'

'I agree it's impossible and you're not psychic.' Gregory's voice deepened and was almost threatening. 'In any case you were in here with me.'

Rena nodded and had barely closed the door when Roger, who immediately noted that she was trembling, was at her side. 'Are you feeling ill? Do you want to go home?'

'No thanks. I'll be fine in a minute' but as Roger guided her back towards her chair Rena discovered that she couldn't stop shaking, and wondered if he had heard Gregory's last remark. She was also aware of Lisa looking at her with curiosity while Sarah's expression was one of resentment but this quickly turned to one of concern as she leant forward and whispered, 'Has Gregory heard about the police appeal? Is that why he was shouting?'

'Probably' said Roger quickly and before Rena could reply. Then, as his gaze travelled from one to the other, 'You've all been very supportive and understanding, for which I'm very grateful however, if there's anything you haven't already told them, you must help the police with their enquiries.'

Roger glanced at Rena again, saw she was still trembling and added, 'I know it's early but I'm sure we would all enjoy some coffee.'

In a flash Lisa was on her feet. 'That's no problem.'

Tessa's confidence ebbed as she entered the hotel wondering how she would find Heather Wingate in such a large impressive foyer then, suddenly she saw her. Tall, slender and wearing a tailored suit in a lovely shade of turquoise the white-haired woman turned when Tessa saw she was holding a copy of Country Life, as arranged. Their gaze met and Tessa moved towards her, 'Mrs. Wingate?'

'Tessa!' There was no doubting the delight in Heather's voice but there were also tears in her eyes as she held Tessa at arm's length. 'Oh my dear, you're so like Irene, your mother.' Tessa nodded and bit her lip. Matthew had said the same thing when he saw Susan's photographs of the christening.

It was some time later, after two cups of coffee apiece and Heather had learnt more details about Jessica's accident that she said, 'So this Amanda Lockwood in Guernsey is really your Amanda?'

Tessa had recounted how Matthew and then Uncle Ben had met Amanda in Exeter and handed over the photographs that Matthew had taken that evening. 'Although the hairstyle is slightly different and he knew it was impossible Matthew thought she was Jessica, while Uncle Ben thought it was me. However, now you can see for yourself.'

Heather held the photograph and nodded. 'On the few occasions that I saw you as babies I couldn't tell you apart and now, looking at this, the likeness is still incredible.'

'I'll be able to tell you more about Amanda when we come back from Guernsey, that is if you're still in Bristol. What are your plans?'

'To stay here, at this hotel, while we look for a house. Arthur could have retired at fifty-five but now, at fifty-seven, feels it's time to come home, to England. This morning he's gone to see an old colleague who's retired and living in Wells, who is thinking of moving to a smaller house. If he does move and we like his present place we might make an offer for it.' Heather had already accepted Tessa's invitation for that evening and continued, 'Arthur will be able to tell you more about it tonight.'

'If it's not suitable I'm sure Roger will be pleased to help you.' Heather then learnt that, due to the agency being short-staffed, Roger was very busy at work however his mother was very supportive.

'That was a really enjoyable evening. They're both charming and very interesting' said Matthew as they watched Heather and Arthur drive away.

'I thought she was very pleasant when I met her this morning. I didn't see Debbie but if she was on duty and saw me I'm sure she'll be curious.'

'And tell Keith.' Matthew looked thoughtful as he helped Tessa unload the dishwasher. 'Would he remember Heather? Did he ever meet her?'

It was Tessa's turn to look pensive. 'The only occasion would have been our christening and to him that was probably just a grown-up party. I doubt that he would remember her. Although Heather's still a good looking woman I'm sure she's changed considerably since then.'

'Is the idea of living in England worrying you?' Heather glanced at Arthur as they emerged from the lift and walked towards their room.

'No, I'm looking forward to it and, if you like the house I saw this morning, living in Wells. It's a lovely area to explore and, once we're settled, I could possibly become involved with a well-deserving charity but that's something we can discuss. However you're looking rather anxious, what's the matter, do you feel ill?'

'No, it's not me. It's about Tessa. I know I've only just met her and she's a lovely young woman but I don't like the idea of her being involved with these police investigations. I realise she's only identified a man who could be connected with the burglaries, but she could be hurt or injured if she met him again.'

'That's highly unlikely. I'm sure she's not in any danger so stop worrying.' Arthur had been pacing to and fro since their return and as he paused Heather sank into a chair by the window and asked, 'What's troubling you?'

'I'll tell you when I've poured the drinks. What would you like?'

'A mineral water, please.'

'It's about those accounts which were opened for the girls.' Arthur handed Heather her glass and after taking a sip of his malt whisky, resumed, 'You were so delighted to receive letters from Tessa and Jessica, to learn they were well and moving into a flat that you brushed aside the fact that you hadn't heard from Amanda.'

'They were only babies at the time so the accounts were opened in their respective names with Laurence and I as their guardians. But he's dead.'

Arthur nodded. 'Exactly. Only Tessa and Jessica went to Margaret and Laurence therefore whatever happened to Amanda occurred about the same time. If Harcourt knew that Amanda had been adopted he should have insisted that Laurence advise you.'

'Why didn't Mr. Harcourt tell Tessa and Jessica they had a sister? If he knew of Amanda's whereabouts he should also have written to her.' Heather hesitated, 'Obviously Amanda in Guernsey hasn't heard from Mr. Harcourt, so what's happened to the bank account?'

'It should still be intact, - unclaimed. It's still hers.'

'And the legacy from the maternal grandparents, which Tessa and Jessica received when they were twenty-one. That was probably a nice little nest-egg.'

'Harcourt should have traced her. If he put the usual notice in the papers Amanda or her adoptive parents would surely have seen it and the girls would have been re-united years ago. It all seems rather strange to me.' And aware that Heather was staring at him open-mouthed, Arthur resumed, 'I don't want to cast aspersions on anyone at this stage but I think we should pay Mr. Harcourt a visit in the morning.'

Meanwhile, in the Redland area, Debbie told Keith, 'I saw Tessa this morning. She was having coffee with one of our residents.'

'Who? What did she look like?' But even when told that the hotel was full Keith persisted, 'Was she young, old?' and when there was no immediate reply, 'Could it have been her old nanny?'

'I don't know why you're so bothered, however she did have white hair.'

'If it was the ex-nanny, why did they meet at the hotel and not Tessa's place?' and without pausing for breath, 'It's a damn nuisance she couldn't mind her own business. She wasn't content with just writing to Tessa, was she? Oh no, she had to visit her, produce photographs and ask questions. Then you weren't much better when Tessa turned up here.'

Debbie shrugged. She knew to her cost, her shoulders and arms were still sore and bruised from the blows Keith had delivered on Monday, that it was better for her to keep quiet.

'Why don't you say something?' asked Keith. 'Afraid I'm going to hit you again?'

Debbie braced herself and recalled that the first time his temper had given way to violence was after his father's death, on learning that - whilst he had inherited the house - there was very little money. Certainly not enough to carry out the necessary repairs and redecoration. Keith had not hit her then but had thrown several plates across the kitchen, smashing them. He had not apologised then, or on any other occasion.

Debbie yawned, she had been on a split shift which finished at half past ten, and was tired. 'I'm going to make myself a hot drink, do you want one?'

'Don't be so damn stupid! You know I don't like anything milky.' This was accompanied by the slamming of a cupboard door, a flow of expletives then, as Debbie reached the kitchen, he called out, 'We're out of whisky. Go and get me a couple of bottles.'

'I'm tired. You want it so you can go for it.' Debbie filled and plugged in the kettle, ignoring the dirty plates that littered the draining board. She had spent the afternoon cleaning the living room, annoyed that she had allowed it to get in such a state and considered that her own appearance on Monday evening had been equally scruffy. It was surprising that Tessa and Matthew had stayed so long, they had probably been disgusted at what they'd seen.

'Where do you keep your money? There isn't enough in your purse' grumbled Keith from the doorway.

'That's all I have.' Holding a mug in one hand and the kettle in the other Debbie turned to look at Keith, thinking that once again he looked untidy and repulsive. A grubby tee-shirt was strained across his chest while dirty jeans emphasised his paunch.

'You're not very good at house-keeping, are you?' Keith's grey eyes glittered angrily. 'You know I always like to keep two bottles of whisky in the house.'

The words 'You're the one who drinks it, why don't you buy it?' sprang to Debbie's lips but, with considerable restraint, she said, 'I'm on the early shift so I'm going to bed.'

CHAPTER TWELVE

Douglas Harcourt was not a happy man, apprehensive as to how he would deal with Heather Wingate and her husband. He had known, years ago, that she would eventually return to Bristol and now that day was here. Although senior partner and fifty-eight, Douglas found himself shaking and muttered, 'My God! What am I going to tell her?' But before he could gather his thoughts there was a knock at the door and Judith, his secretary, told him, 'Mr. and Mrs. Wingate are here.'

'Thank you. Show them in, please.' While his mind whirled with chaotic thoughts about the Wingates, Douglas' gaze lingered on Judith, an attractive and curvaceous woman in her mid forties, an excellent secretary and marvellous in bed.

For a brief moment Douglas felt he would be able to deal with any questions raised by Heather Wingate but these hopes were quickly dismissed by the glint in the eyes of the tall broad-shouldered man who followed her. The slim white-haired woman who entered the room had an air of self-assurance and Douglas immediately realised that she would want to know the truth. Despite years spent in humid climates Arthur Wingate was still an incredibly handsome man, deep blue eyes emphasised his slightly tanned features, silver grey hair and moustache.

'I'm sure, although you were Jessica's godmother, Tessa is glad you're here' said Douglas once they had all shaken hands and were seated. 'Tessa must still be devastated. I only spoke to her briefly at the funeral, and again after the reading of the Will. Such a tragedy.'

'That's not the only one.' Arthur's expression and voice were grim and Douglas glanced at Heather for enlightenment.

'What do you mean?' asked the solicitor.

'You may not know or remember that Irene and Richard were my best friends. When I attended the christening, left England and later arranged with Laurence for the bank accounts, there were three children.'

It was at this point that Arthur intervened. 'What's happened to Amanda? And what's happened about the account in her name? There must be a considerable balance.'

'Amanda is more important than the money' cut in Heather. 'Until recently Tessa thought Jessica was her only sister. Is Amanda dead and if so, why didn't Laurence let me know? Why didn't he advise me to stop payments to the account in her name?' Heather didn't even glance at Arthur aware that he, like her, was watching Douglas Harcourt squirm uncomfortably in his chair.

'Laurence ...'

'What are you trying to tell me? That Laurence knew, but he's been dead for three years so I presume he told you.'

'Why didn't he and Margaret take Amanda as well as Tessa and Jessica?' Arthur's eyes glittered dangerously as he continued. 'You knew there were three accounts, didn't you think it strange that neither Tessa nor Jessica referred to Amanda?'

Douglas looked from one to the other and nervously moistened his lips. 'I .. I don't know.'

'Oh come now, Mr. Harcourt. You're a solicitor, probably a family man ...' the shriek that was uttered startled both Heather and Arthur but this did not deter the latter who, in a low but persuasive voice, repeated, 'What happened to Amanda?'

At that moment the door was flung open, Judith rushed in and ran towards Douglas. 'Darling, are you all right? I heard you shout' and glaring at Arthur, 'what's happening?'

'This is a business meeting between Mr. Harcourt and ourselves, hardly any concern of yours.'

'Anything that upsets Douglas is my concern.'

Douglas nodded. 'Judith is more than my secretary. We've been together for twenty years' and glancing at Judith he told her, 'I'll be fine my dear. We're just discussing the Morgan girls.'

At this Judith shook her head and snapped angrily, 'You stupid old fool! You haven't told them the truth about Amanda and ...' her voice faded as she fell to her knees at his side and whispered, 'Oh my God! What have I said?'

Arthur reached for and held Heather's hand as the veneer of this supposedly efficient and smartly-dressed woman disintegrated before their eyes. Her make-up was now blotchy, her eye-shadow and lipstick suddenly became garish while, as she slowly rose to her feet, her jacket was strained across her ample bosom while her skirt rode up revealing flabby thighs. Arthur waited a moment while she smoothed her now-creased black skirt over her ample hips and straightened her jacket then he said, 'I think you'd better sit down and enlighten us.'

Judith glanced at Douglas who was still staring at her open-mouthed. 'Shall I?'

Douglas blinked, sat up straight and nodded. 'Join us, yes. But leave the explanation to me. This could take some time so could you organise some coffee, please.'

As the door closed Heather leant forward. 'Before you start on what might be a lengthy explanation, what happened to Amanda, where is she?'

'She ..she was adopted. Laurence was furious. The first thing he knew about it was when he arrived home to find only Tessa and Jessica when there should have been three of them. Margaret hadn't mentioned that she was thinking about doing this, - she obviously knew he would forbid it.' Douglas looked at Arthur. 'I shouldn't say this but Margaret Morgan was a very unpleasant woman. A real bitch! Laurence came to see me the next morning. He was in a terrible state. Margaret refused to tell him how she had achieved this so quickly and wouldn't even discuss...'

'Why didn't Margaret and Laurence move into Richard's house?' interrupted Heather. 'It was large enough to accommodate them, the three children and they could have kept Susan.' And when Douglas looked blank, 'Margaret knew I was Irene's best friend, why didn't one of them 'phone me about the accident. Why did they leave it to you to tell me? I would have flown back for the funeral, we could have discussed the children's future. If I had known what she intended to do I would quite happily have returned to care for the children, with Susan's help, instead of them being split up.'

Aware of the pressure of Arthur's hand on hers, they had agreed that neither would refer to Susan's sudden re-appearance or the reason for Tessa's visit to Guernsey, Heather asked, 'What happened to the account in Amanda's name?' And, as Judith entered carrying a loaded tray, Heather continued, 'Why, although he didn't have any details, didn't Laurence tell me about Amanda being adopted when we discussed the bank accounts.'

'I don't know' said Douglas.

'I think he was still upset that Margaret had taken such a drastic step without even consulting him' interjected Judith.

'So Amanda, wherever she is, has no knowledge of this account?'

'Or the legacy from her maternal grandparents. And this was quite substantial' offered Douglas. 'Tessa and Jessica received theirs when they were twenty-one.'

On learning that Margaret would probably have veto-ed any attempt to trace Amanda, Heather said, 'Laurence could have tried after she died.'

'He certainly didn't mention it and was always anxious to impart his problems. Unfortunately Keith, his son, was one of them. Apparently he was an objectionable child and openly resented his cousins' presence in the house. For some reason Margaret spoilt him with the result that he's grown up to be an even more objectionable adult.'

'Keith' repeated Heather thoughtfully. 'I only met him once, at the girls' christening. Is he a bright young man? Where does he work?'

'He's a car salesman. He did his apprenticeship as a mechanic but after working at the same garage for some time decided he was tired of getting his hands dirty.' Douglas added more sugar and stirred his coffee. 'I've only met Keith on one occasion, after Laurence's funeral. He wasn't very happy or satisfied at the reading of the Will when he learnt that although he inherited the house, there wasn't much money.'

'Then he 'phoned you last week asking about Jessica's Will' said Judith.

Douglas nodded. 'He wanted to know why he hadn't heard from me, received the usual letter, and then had the audacity to ask how much she had left him.' Heather and Arthur knew that Keith had questioned Tessa about Jessica's Will. 'He wasn't very happy to learn he wasn't included, in fact he was very rude.'

'His language was disgusting when he 'phoned Douglas' interrupted Judith.

'What do you intend to do about Amanda?' asked Heather. 'You were aware of her existence, surely you must have been curious about her whereabouts?'

'You met Tessa and Jessica twice yet you never told them about Amanda' said Arthur.

'It wasn't for me to do that.'

'Stuff and nonsense. I'm sure they would have asked you to trace her if they had known of her existence. In fact, I'm surprised she didn't come forward when the notice about the grandparents' Will was published.' Arthur stopped abruptly, 'You did do that?'

'I .. er' Douglas looked blank when Heather said, 'Amanda is entitled to the money in that account, and the legacy. She may be in need of it.' Heather and Arthur had discussed Amanda and their forthcoming interview with Douglas on the way to his office and whilst they knew of Amanda's whereabouts, which they did not intend to reveal, they were both determined that Douglas Harcourt should be made aware of Laurence's and his own shortcomings.

Douglas' gaze travelled to Judith and back to Heather but there was still no reply so she persisted, 'I understand that the Salvation Army are very good at finding people.'

'Details. They'll want details' mumbled Douglas.

'That's not difficult. You know the date of birth, which is the same as Tessa's and Jessica's, and approximately when Amanda was adopted. You know that Tessa and Jessica look alike so probably Amanda is identical, therefore you have a description. If they ask any other questions I'm sure you'll be able to answer them. Just think of Tessa's re-action when you tell her you've found Amanda.'

'More like a ruddy shock, if you ask me' said Judith. 'Fancy being confronted with a sister you didn't know existed, after all these years.'

Heather was aware of Arthur nudging her and stood up. 'It would be a shock for both of them. However we'll leave the matter with you and look forward to hearing of any developments. You have our address and 'phone number.'

'Harcourt's really worried' said Arthur a few minutes later as they stood on the pavement.

'Serve him right. I've been in touch with him over the years and he never told me that Amanda had been adopted. It's strange that so much has happened so quickly since Jessica's death. Matthew meeting Amanda, and then Susan, the ex-nanny, writing to Tessa. Although she and I knew that there were three of them, the only people who'll have any details of the adoption will be Hazel and Bruce Maybury.'

'And you'll have to wait until next week when Tessa returns from Guernsey to hear about those. Anyhow I'm thirsty. Let's find a pub.'

CHAPTER THIRTEEN

'I'm nervous.' Tessa stopped suddenly and looked at Matthew for re-assurance. 'Do you think we've done the right thing coming here? When do I tell Amanda about the bank account in her name, and the legacy from our grandparents?'

'That's something you can't rush. I suggest you wait for a suitable opportunity.' Matthew slid his arm round Tessa's waist. 'If this evening doesn't work out we'll enjoy the remainder of the week-end on our own. Anyhow there's time for a quick drink if you need some dutch courage' and when Tessa nodded, 'There's a bar opposite Reception.'

However this was not necessary, for no sooner had they reached the foyer than a young woman appeared in the doorway and Tessa gasped. For a moment Amanda just stared at Tessa, regardless of her husband and parents standing behind her, all looking rather apprehensive.

Hazel Maybury clutched her husband's arm and whispered, 'If it wasn't for the different hairstyles and clothes you couldn't tell them apart.' It was as Tim muttered, 'My God!' that the two young women slowly approached each other, staring, and then Tessa held out her arms.

'Why did you look at Amanda's arm?' Hazel had studied the photographs that Susan had given Tessa and listened to a resume of Susan's visit as they drank their aperitifs but now, as they waited for their main course, she could no longer contain her curiosity.

'To look at the moles on her arm.' Tessa smiled, aware that this kind warm-hearted person who had loved and cared for Amanda must be finding it all very confusing. 'Susan noticed we all had four moles on our arms, in different places, and thought it was another way of identifying us.'

'How clever! Where are yours?'

'On my left arm, same as Amanda's. But hers are below her elbow while mine are above.' Tessa pushed back her sleeve to reveal the four moles which formed a circle. 'Jessica's were on her right arm, in exactly the same place as Amanda's.'

'Susan must have been very upset when she had to leave you all.'

Tessa nodded and turned towards Amanda who, glancing at Matthew said, 'It was the expression on your face as you came towards me that captured my attention. I was afraid you were going to have a heart attack.' And transferring her gaze to Tim, 'It wasn't until we reached Matthew's hotel that either of us relaxed.'

Matthew nodded. 'I couldn't believe my eyes and I can see that Tim is the same.'

Tim, who was very tall with sandy coloured hair, grinned at Tessa. 'I'm sorry if I appear rude. Seeing you and Amanda standing side by side was so incredible, plus the fact that neither of you had known of the other's existence.'

'We were only eighteen months old at the time of the accident. I suppose Jessica and I were upset when we didn't see our parents, Amanda or our nanny and were taken to a smaller house. As we grew older we asked about our parents but Aunt Margaret wasn't very informative.' Tessa looked at Hazel. 'Did you ever meet her?'

'No. As you know we were living in Bath at the time and it was the vicar from our church who contacted us. He knew that we, and several other couples in his parish, wanted to adopt a child and had mentioned this to a colleague in Bristol. We were only told that the parents had died in a car crash and that the only relative, an elderly aunt unknown to the vicar in Bristol, would not be able to cope with a young child.'

Hazel noticed Tessa's eyes fill with tears and decided there was no need for her to know the truth that, two days later, Amanda had been found on the vicarage doorstep. Amongst a change of clothing was an envelope containing the Birth Certificate. Unable to trace the elderly aunt the vicar's wife had cared for Amanda while the necessary arrangements were made. 'Amanda settled in and we were all very happy.'

Bruce had listened to Tessa's earlier description of meeting Susan and Heather Wingate with interest, noted her change of expression and now said, 'I think it's marvellous the way you're coping with everything that has happened in such a short time.'

'It has been rather difficult but Matthew has been wonderful and his Uncle Ben is leaning on his Chief Inspector friend.'

Tim knew about the suspicious circumstances surrounding the car crash and leant forward. 'Have the police any idea as to exactly what happened?' Then, seeing that Matthew was puzzled, he explained, 'I'm in the local force, hence the interest.'

'Tim's a sergeant in our C.I.D.' said Amanda proudly.

'Congratulations! You must be doing well. Do you...' Tessa stopped suddenly as Matthew, who was seated opposite her, kicked her foot under the table and Bruce said, 'It was you who replaced the elderly bearded gentleman on the antique programme, wasn't it?' And when Tessa nodded, 'The first time I saw you I thought what's Amanda, who is also very interested in antiques, doing there but I knew that was impossible. However, you've a remarkable knowledge of antiques and you obviously enjoy it.'

'I do and,' aware of Matthew's foot pressing against hers, 'everyone is so friendly.'

'Are you talking about antiques?' Amanda leant forward and looking at Tessa said, 'I usually watch that programme but pay more attention to the antiques than the experts. Snuff boxes must be very interesting. I haven't seen many but sometimes there are some in the shop on the right hand side as you go towards High Street.'

'Thanks. I'll have a look in the morning when we explore St. Peter Port.'

'I had no idea you had such lovely scenery' said Tessa as she and Amanda stood on the path gazing at the steep gorse-covered cliffs and the bay far below. 'In fact, I must admit I really don't know very much about the island.'

'It's a good place to live. There are disadvantages but that applies wherever you live. My parents have been very happy here, I received an excellent education, the local people are very friendly and we've all made a lot of friends.'

Tessa nodded, she had experienced this herself when walking through town that morning. 'A number of people greeted me while others commented on the weather or a recent concert, obviously thinking I was you. I'm afraid I didn't say I wasn't you - it would have taken too long.' Tessa paused and her expression became sombre as she asked, 'Did you ever think about your natural parents? Want to know more about them, or wonder if you had any other relatives?'

'If I'd known the truth and I can't blame my adoptive parents for that, - yes, I would. When Hazel gave me my Birth Certificate there was nothing to indicate I was one of triplets. I was registered as Amanda, daughter of Irene and Richard Morgan. Like Hazel and Bruce I thought Gilmour was my father's second name. The surname wasn't hyphenated. Although Hazel and Bruce enjoy music and attend a number of concerts at St. James, it never occurred to them that my natural father was the late Richard Gilmour-Morgan, the concert pianist. It was only when I looked at my Birth

Certificate on that Thursday evening and recalled that conversation, that it all fell into place. I realise Hazel told you about the elderly aunt who couldn't have coped with a young child, so there was nothing to suggest there could be any other relatives. As I've already told you, I had a happy childhood but I did feel something was missing.'

Amanda grinned and linked her arm through Tessa's. 'The news that I've a sister' and a shadow passing over her face, 'that we were triplets, will soon be general knowledge.' Then, pointing to two figures on the beach who were waving frantically and then bending to pull off their shoes and socks, 'Look, Tim's persuaded Matthew to go in the water.' And seeing Tessa's concern, 'It won't be cold and they've got the climb up all those steps afterwards.

Tessa watched as Matthew followed Tim's example, rolling up his jeans and venturing out until they were ankle deep in the water. It seemed to Tessa that this was a good opportunity to tell Amanda about the bank account and indicating the bench she said, 'Shall we sit down?'

Amanda's expression was anxious as she gazed at Tessa. 'Is there something else you have to tell me?'

'Yes, but there's no need to look so worried.' Amanda already knew that Heather Wingate had been Jessica's godmother and that Tessa had only recently met her.

Amanda's eyes widened as she learnt that Jessica and Tessa had used the balance of their bank accounts when they were eighteen, when they moved into a flat and later, some of the legacy from their maternal grandparents but that the account in her name, and the legacy, were untouched. 'Why me?' whispered Amanda.

'You're our sister. As you heard last night, Aunt Margaret didn't even tell her husband, Uncle Laurence, what she had done. It was your mother, who I think is a really lovely person, who filled in the details. Heather and our grandparents thought we were all together.'

'It's incredible. If Susan hadn't written and visited you, we wouldn't be sat here now. However, despite that, I still don't feel entitled to the money.'

'But you are and I'm sure Tim and your parents would agree.'

'I'll talk to them about it. Anyhow, if you don't mind talking about her, tell me more about Jessica. What's her husband like? How is he coping?'

Amanda had seen a photograph of Jessica and Roger the previous evening and Tessa told her, 'Naturally he was devastated, however Gregory, his employer has gone to pieces so, in addition to doing his own and Jessica's work, Roger has taken charge of the agency. His mother is very supportive and offered to move in but understood that he preferred to be on his own, knowing that Roger is capable of looking after himself.'

'It's strange that you both met your husbands through your work.'

'Yes. Unfortunately we weren't allowed to have piano lessons which might, if we'd been good enough, have led to a musical career. We were both keen but Aunt Margaret was a proper curmudgeon about it and whilst we knew Uncle Laurence would have agreed, she would have over-ridden his decision.'

'Poor man. She sounds a proper battle-axe, a real horror.'

Tessa nodded. 'She was and Keith was just as bad. Always making snide remarks. He's still the same. At least we had each other and possibly became even closer. However, when the time came we agreed it would be sensible to take a secretarial course. Jessica's interest is music was greater than mine and she started piano lessons at twenty-one, using some of her legacy. Later, Olivia, her mother-in-law, who had attended all the concerts in which our parents appeared, gave her a piano as a personal wedding present.'

Tessa and Amanda gazed at each other, both on the verge of tears and Amanda, who knew that Matthew's parents died several years ago, noted the wistfulness in Tessa's voice. 'I liked Uncle Ben. He's quite a character.'

'He's been very kind to me, and Jessica, over the years. I'm very fond of him.' Tessa managed a tremulous smile. 'And now we've found you!'

'What steps are your police taking to trace the perpetrators of these burglaries?' Tim looked at Matthew as they paused for breath. Although he considered himself fit Tim found the steps up from Petit Port to the cliff path hard going. He and other members of the local force had heard about the robberies soon after they started.

'Unfortunately no clues have been found in the houses or grounds where these burglaries occurred and none of the items stolen were on the computer system which is also linked to the Art and Antique Squad at New Scotland Yard.' Tim already knew about the 'phone call and that Tessa had identified the caller as the same man who had approached her, demanding addresses, the previous autumn. 'However Inspector Kershaw and his team are returning to these areas with copies of the photograph that was taken when he approached Tessa last autumn.' Matthew turned to look back over the bay. 'It must be an artist's paradise.'

'Hi, you two! Are you still chatting?' called out Tim as they reached the path and in an undertone to Matthew who was a few paces behind, panting, 'Just look at them. Have you ever seen anything so marvellous?'

CHAPTER FOURTEEN

'I realise it's many years since we stayed in Bristol and there have certainly been many changes in the city, including the rebuilding of this hotel.'

'Yes, architects have become very imaginative.' Roger followed Arthur's gaze around the restaurant. 'I've only seen the foyer on the occasions that I've picked up clients, and this is certainly very spacious.' Roger had not been surprised to hear from Heather, - Tessa had told him that the Wingates were in Bristol and would like to meet him - and had agreed to join them for dinner.

The hotel, situated near the Centre and cathedral, was popular with tourists and business men and now, having enjoyed a salad of crispy vegetables with a pastis dressing and watching the waiters deftly serve the main course, Roger knew he would be able to recommend the Palm Court Restaurant to future clients. Arthur and Heather had both expressed their sympathy and just enquired about the progress made by the police.

'I don't know if there's been any response to their appeal' replied Roger.

'Surely any witnesses at the scene of the accident have been questioned?' hazarded Heather.

'Yes, they were. However, this was asking if anyone had been seen loitering in the parking space behind the agency on the Friday afternoon. Jessica's car was amongst those parked there.'

'Was that the car she was driving ...' Heather's voice faded.

'Yes. The agency car was at the garage.' As he spoke the colour drained from Roger's face and his gaze travelled to Arthur and back to Heather. 'Oh my God! I've just remembered. Gregory asked me to go out to the property at Chew Valley on that Saturday morning, instead of Jessica.'

'Obviously you didn't. Why?'

'Jessica had been dealing with these clients, the Bakers, and it such a lovely morning I thought she should show them this rather unique property, and clinch the deal.'

'Could you have prevented the crash if you'd been driving?' enquired Arthur.

'It's possible.' Roger then recounted that all the staff had heard Gregory's new instructions and, although Jessica had not resented that he should go instead of her, she had later expressed her disappointment. He also told them of the Chief Inspector's call that morning, that the Mechanical Scientist's report stated that the brakes had definitely been tampered with, hence the accident. 'Jessica shouldn't have died' said Roger and stumbling over the next words, 'It .. it was meant for me.'

'I realise you've only just remembered but this could make a difference to the police enquiries' said Arthur, dismissing the multitude of questions that sprang to mind.

'I'll ring Chief Inspector Fowler on Monday.' Roger suddenly discovered he was still holding his knife and fork and placed these across his plate.

'I'm sure he won't mind if you 'phone him tomorrow, or even tonight' said Arthur.

Roger nodded and stood up. 'If you'll excuse me for a few minutes I'll do that now.'

'I'm seeing him in the morning.' Roger's cheeks were flushed as he sat down. 'He sounded really angry that I hadn't told him about this on Tuesday or even when he 'phoned me this morning.'

'Don't let it spoil your evening.' Heather handed Roger the dessert menu. 'You've told him and he'll hear any details in the morning.'

'Thank you. You're very understanding.

It was as they ate their caramelised orange parfait, they had all chosen the same, that Roger learnt about the property in Wells when he said 'If your friend changes his mind and I can help in any way, please let me know.'

'We should know by the end of the week. However, is there any way we can help you during what must be, a difficult time?'

'It's very kind of you to offer but no thanks. My mother is very supportive and understands that I don't want her to move in. Fortunately I'm busy at work. Gregory isn't well, can't concentrate, won't discuss a replacement for .. for Jessica so I'm doing most of his work and dealing with any clients she had, in addition to mine.'

'It's a pity you didn't tell us about this when the accident occurred. It would have saved us a lot of time if we'd known that you were supposed to be driving the car.' Chief Inspector Fowler's voice was grim but despite this he reached for his mug of coffee.

'I'm sorry. I completely forgot, - it was probably due to shock.'

'So, why didn't you drive out to that property.'

'Jessica had dealt with the Bakers, shown them other properties and having seen this one I guessed they'd go for it. I felt she should have the benefit of clinching the deal.' Roger paused but only for a moment. 'As you know, the clients were already at the house and, whilst it's not relevant to your enquiries, they've bought it.'

'Did Gregory handle it?'

'No, I did. He comes in every day but as I've already told you, he's not well.'

Fowler's manner had been brusque when he arrived but this mellowed as he considered that Roger was very loyal. He also knew that, in addition to his own work, Roger was doing most of Gregory's. His thoughts then turned to Rena, Sarah and Lisa who were all unable to think of anyone who disliked Jessica and now it would be interesting to hear their comments about Roger.

In reply to his next query Fowler learnt that Sarah had popped out for some cakes, it was her birthday, which they had enjoyed with their cup of tea. Roger was uncertain how long she was out. Gregory had also gone out and again Roger didn't know for how long. Then, before Fowler could comment Roger said, 'I find it difficult to believe that either of them tampered with Jessica's car and, talking of that, have you had any response to your appeal?'

'We've had the usual time-wasters. Two 'phoned in yesterday. They're calling at the station to-morrow. They both sounded sensible so hopefully we might learn something useful.'

'Bruce and I are still amazed about the bank account in Amanda's name' said Hazel. 'Mrs. Wingate must be very rich.'

'She's a warm-hearted, charming woman who prefers to be called by her christian name, Heather. She's also very attractive' said Matthew.

'Wasn't she Jessica's god-mother?' This came from Tim who had crossed the lawn to join in the discussion but before Matthew could reply Hazel resumed, 'Then there's the legacy from the maternal grandparents. Amanda is still over-whelmed, feels she isn't really entitled to it.'

'I'm quite capable of supporting Amanda. In fact there's no need for her to work but she enjoys it' said Tim.

It was Sunday afternoon, they had all enjoyed a barbecue in the Maybury's garden and Matthew looked towards Amanda and Tessa who were at the bottom of the garden where the former was pointing out the border of multi-coloured mesembryanthemums and said, 'The bank account and legacy are in Amanda's name. Douglas Harcourt, the solicitor, should have put the usual notice in the papers asking Amanda to contact him. Heather 'phoned us before we left on Friday to say they were going to see him later that morning. They had no intention of telling him about my chance meeting with Amanda in Exeter, or that we were coming to Guernsey but no doubt they left him with something to think about. I'm sure we'll hear all the details when we return to-morrow.'

'What's the usual procedure? Will the fact that Amanda lives in Guernsey make any difference to her claiming the bank balance and legacy?' asked Hazel.

'No, it should be quite straight forward' replied Matthew and then elaborated, 'She'll have to produce her Birth Certificate, if she hasn't got that a copy can be easily obtained, and her Marriage Certificate. She will probably need any adoption papers however I'll let you know about that.'

'Amanda does have her Birth Certificate. Apart from a change of clothes that was the only thing ....' Bruce stopped abruptly as Hazel, determined that he didn't say anything about Amanda being left on the vicarage doorstep, suddenly exclaimed, 'Look at that greedy seagull! We cleared up completely but he's still looking for scraps.'

CHAPTER FIFTEEN

'Oh no, not you again!' groaned Gregory Niven as he opened the front door.

'Can we have a word, sir?' and before Gregory could protest Detective Inspector Fowler and Detective Sergeant Branch were already in the hall and following him to the kitchen.

'Can't this wait, I'm already late.'

Fowler noted the patches of stubble, evidence of a hit-and-miss attempt at shaving and that Gregory looked bleary-eyed. 'No it can't. Why didn't you tell me you asked Roger to drive out to Chew Valley on that Saturday morning?'

Gregory scrunched a half-eaten slightly burnt slice of toast and picked up a mug of coffee. 'He didn't go so it wasn't relevant.'

'That's where you're wrong, surely you can see that. If the perpetrator wanted Roger out of the way but Jessica died instead ...' Fowler's voice faded as Gregory rushed past him and then came the sound of retching from the downstairs cloakroom.

'That wasn't exactly successful' commented Branch five minutes later as he fastened his seat-belt.

'I thought it was rather enlightening.'

'Do you really think Gregory did it? That he's still in love with Jessica and wanted Roger out of the way? But now the wrong person's dead.'

'That might account for his general appearance and current lack of interest in the business. We know that he left his office, ostensibly to fetch some papers from his car so hopefully we'll learn more when we call at the agency. The Super wasn't very happy on Friday. Ben Ormerod had been on the 'phone to him. Apparently they occasionally play golf and

Ben thinks that gives him some leverage when it comes to expecting results, but even now there isn't anything to report.'

Fowler glared at Branch as though it was his fault. The first caller had seen a young man sitting in a large white car, this was obviously Keith, drive away while the second had noticed two men talking. Although the descriptions were vague, these were Keith and Gregory. There had been other 'phone calls but these had been from people who merely walked on the opposite pavement, engrossed in conversation.

'The appeal is being repeated today. Hopefully we might get something more definite.' Branch spoke quietly but despite this Fowler stood up immediately. 'We can't sit around waiting for that. Let's go and see the girls at the agency.'

Sarah and Lisa exchanged curious glances as Detective Inspector Fowler and his sergeant followed Rena into Roger's office. It was convenient that Roger was out with clients and that his office could be used for the purpose of further interrogation but they were both concerned that this was necessary.

'Why didn't you tell me that Gregory asked Roger to go out to the property at Chew Valley on that Saturday morning, Miss Lessiter?' Fowler had seated himself in Roger's chair and looked directly at Rena.

'I didn't think it was important. Jessica went as previously arranged.'

'Didn't it occur to you that Roger could have been the victim instead of Jessica?'

'No. At the time I was so shocked about Jessica that I couldn't think of anything else. I still find it difficult to concentrate. Why should anyone want to harm Jessica, or Roger?'

'I'm hoping you can tell me the answer to that.' Fowler's voice was low and persuasive. 'You've worked for

Gregory Niven since he started this business, have there been any affairs or relationships amongst the staff?'

'Gregory was surprised, maybe even upset, when Jessica and Roger announced their engagement.' Fowler then learnt that, prior to Roger joining the agency, Gregory had taken Jessica out on several occasions. If jealous, Gregory hadn't shown it and had attended the wedding. Rena didn't know if he was seeing anyone at the moment but she was concerned at his lack of interest in the business and his unkempt appearance.

It was Branch who asked the next question which produced a nod of approval from Fowler and a surprised expression on Rena's face. However, after a moment's hesitation she told him that Roger had taken Sarah Mortimer out on several occasions, but that Sarah had not shown any animosity or resentment when he transferred his attention to Jessica.

'I didn't think any of them were very forthcoming, did you, sir?' Branch glanced at the Inspector as they waited for the traffic lights to turn green.

'No.' Fowler looked thoughtful as he considered that Lisa and Sarah had heard Gregory's new instructions and apologised for omitting this when previously questioned. The possibility that Roger could have been the victim had not occurred to either of them but Sarah in particular, had looked shocked. Their answer to his next question had been the same as Rena's. Neither of them knew anyone who disliked Roger sufficiently to harm or injure him.

'Did you notice Sarah's expression when we questioned her?' asked Fowler.

'Yes. It was as though she was in a daze. Perhaps she's hoping Roger will turn to her again,' ventured Branch.

'Did you meet her? Is she like you? Did you have a good time?' enquired Heather so quickly that Arthur grinned and shook his head despairingly.

'We thoroughly enjoyed ourselves. They were all so friendly and hospitable that I felt as though I've always known them.'

'But you haven't answered my question about Amanda' persisted Heather.

'Really, my dear, you've hardly given Tessa a moment to breathe. However, let's order some drinks, decide what we're eating and then you can listen to your heart's content.'

On their return home that morning, neither Tessa nor Matthew were surprised to find a message from Heather suggesting that they meet for lunch. Although anxious to have a lengthier and more detailed account of their meeting with Amanda and her parents, Heather agreed to wait until the following afternoon when Susan, who had 'phoned later that morning and was also interested to hear about Amanda, was driving up to Bristol.

It wasn't until Tessa had told Heather of the various people who had mistaken her for Amanda on Saturday morning when they walked through St. Peter Port that she stopped suddenly and, looking at Arthur, she apologised. 'I'm sorry. I haven't even asked about your meeting with Mr. Harcourt.'

'There's no hurry, my dear,' and his deep blue eyes twinkling, Arthur continued, 'It's good to know you enjoyed yourselves. However we did meet Douglas Harcourt and his rather glamorous secretary Judith, who startled us by rushing in, and her subsequent outburst. It was later that we both admitted we were puzzled by Judith's comment, "You haven't told them the truth about Amanda", with the result that we visited the bank.'

Arthur picked up his glass and looked at Tessa. 'As you know Laurence was immediately appointed your guardian and later Heather was appointed joint guardian. She was therefore able to make enquiries about the account in Amanda's name.'

Matthew noted Arthur's hesitation and took the opportunity to ask, 'Is there anything untoward about it?'

'No. Laurence's name had naturally been deleted from the account and the assistant manager to whom we spoke said they were surprised that, when questioned as to why Amanda had not turned up, Laurence reluctantly confessed he didn't know where she was.' Arthur paused and looked at Matthew, 'We know that was the truth. That his wife had never told him what she had arranged for Amanda, but the bank officials must have been rather disgusted that, as her uncle, he had never attempted to find her. According to the young man to whom we spoke, they contacted Douglas Harcourt at the time when he said he would try to trace Amanda but even now, seven years later, he is still saying the same thing. I'm surprised they didn't take any positive action themselves.'

'So they'll all be amazed when Amanda does get in touch' said Tessa.

'When does she intend to do that?' asked Heather and on hearing that Amanda would probably be writing to Mr. Harcourt and the bank within the next few days, she said 'Surely they'll want to meet her in person.'

'Amanda and Tim are hoping to come over during the summer holidays unless they can arrange time off together before then.'

Arthur nodded. 'That's good. However I would like to know what Judith meant.'

Heather looked thoughtful. 'The bank account is in order, the balance is what it should be, in other words no money has been withdrawn so what else could it be?'

'Perhaps Judith was referring to the fact that Harcourt had not inserted the necessary notices in the papers regarding the grandparents' Will' suggested Tessa.

'Judith was certainly excited' and aware that Matthew and Arthur were looking concerned, Heather asked, 'Is there something else we don't know?'

'We'll give Harcourt until Wednesday and if we don't hear anything from him by then we'll phone...'

Arthur paused as two waiters placed plates of spaghetti bolognaise in front of them and Tessa took advantage of this, 'I haven't told you another interesting item of news' and aware of Heather and Arthur's curiosity, 'Amanda is interested in antiques and, when she's not teaching, enjoys attending local auctions. There's some lovely old houses in the island ....'

'Never mind about those' interrupted Heather. 'Do you know if there have been any developments since last Wednesday? Did Inspector Kershaw tell you what...'

'Really, my dear,' said Arthur. 'Do you seriously think he would tell Tessa what they intend to do. However, I would like to hear more about Guernsey.'

'It's a lovely island.' Matthew grinned, 'But until you become accustomed to it, the water's rather cold.' Then seeing Heather's surprise, 'No, I didn't swim. Tim and I only put our feet in at Petit Port, which is on the south coast. The beaches on the west coast are more accessible. We saw those on Sunday morning when Tim took us on an island tour.'

'It sounds as though you became instant friends,' observed Arthur.

Tessa shook her head as Matthew reached for the receiver. They had been instructed to let it ring three times before answering and that she should answer all calls. It was about the same time that she had received the ominous call the previous Tuesday and her voice was shaky. Relief flooded through her as Roger spoke. 'Tessa, are you all right?'

'Yes .. yes thank you, Roger. How are you?'

'Fine but there's something you should know.'

'Come round and join us for supper. It's only quiche and salad but you're very welcome.'

'So you only remembered that on Saturday evening' said Matthew half an hour later, after Roger had recounted his 'phone call, Fowler's subsequent visit and interrogation on Sunday morning.

'Yes, and he told me off on both occasions.'

Tessa was still wide-eyed as she asked, 'So what happens now?'

'Assuming that I was the intended victim he's questioning everyone again and will probably visit you.'

Roger knew about Tessa's visit to the police station and looked at her across the table. 'Have the police had any further results?'

'Not to our knowledge. We only came back from Guernsey this morning.'

'Of course! And I haven't even asked how you got on, if you enjoyed yourselves?' A few minutes later Roger gazed at the photographs taken of Amanda and Tessa sitting on the cliff path and in the Maybury's garden, 'You're so alike' he murmured but it was obvious he was thinking of Jessica then, looking at Tessa he asked, 'Is she really your Amanda?'

'Yes, her Birth Certificate has the same details and she has the four moles on her arm, exactly as described by Susan. She's a piano teacher, loves music and is also interested in antiques.' Tessa paused and then asked, 'Would you like some more coffee?' but before she could pick up the coffee pot the 'phone rang and she glanced at Matthew, who nodded.

The two men watched as Tessa picked up the receiver and then, her hand over the mouthpiece, she whispered, 'It's Keith.'

'I wonder what he wants?' muttered Matthew.

'Probably money' said Roger in an undertone and the next moment Tessa said adamantly, 'No, I can't lend you £5,000.'

'My God! He's got a nerve' said Roger.

'Even if he does the repairs and decorates the house himself he'll need more than that.' Matthew was moving towards Tessa when her voice suddenly became icy. 'Are you threatening me, Keith? And yes, I do know what happened to Jessica. You might consider yourself very clever however the police aren't stupid and if you persist in boasting about your mechanical capabilities....' Tessa slammed the receiver down, glared at it and turning to Matthew said, 'I need a drink. A strong one, please.'

'What does he want all that money for?' asked Matthew after Tessa has gulped down half the contents of her glass, aware that Roger was also curious.

'Gambling debts and, as you can both probably guess, he turned really nasty.'

'And you weren't the only person who heard him' said Roger, who knew that all their incoming calls were being monitored.

Matthew slid his arm around Tessa's shoulders and gazing at her reached up and wound a strand of hair around his finger. 'What did he say when he threatened you?'

'He called me some horrible names and then said, "and don't forget I'm your next-of-kin".'

'The bastard! I'll make sure Inspector Fowler hears about this' said Matthew.

'I expect Inspector Kershaw will do that' said Tessa, at the same time disentangling her hair from Matthew's finger then, as Roger finished his drink and stood up, 'There's no need for you to rush off, is there?'

'We are busy and there's no sign of Gregory showing any interest in the business.' Roger bent to kiss Tessa's cheek. 'Don't worry about Keith, we'll sort him out' but as he reached the front door Roger's expression became sombre and he told Matthew, 'Keep your car and garage locked, at home and at work.'

Matthew looked aghast. 'My God, you really mean it.'

Roger nodded. 'Better to be safe than sorry.'

'What's the matter, are you worried about Keith's conversation?'

Tessa stopped suddenly and looked at Matthew as he stood in the doorway. She had been pacing to and fro since he left the room with Roger and now said, 'Not for myself but for Debbie. Keith was so horrible he'll probably turn on her when she gets home, and knock her about.'

'Perhaps she was there when he 'phoned.'

'I don't think he would have used such foul language if she was. Anyhow I'm going to 'phone the hotel to warn her. She may decide to stay with a friend.'

'That won't improve Keith's temper.'

'I realise that but it's better than Debbie being abused.'

'Oh Lord!' exclaimed Debbie two minutes later. 'I'm sorry I wasn't there to stop Keith bothering you.'

Tessa had not elaborated on the full content of the conversation and she did not intend to do so instead she said, 'I don't think you should go back there tonight. Could you stay with a friend?'

'Yes but I'll go back tomorrow when he's gone to work, to pack some clothes. I'm having a week off, going to see my parents.'

'I'm sure they'll be thrilled to see you. Have a lovely time.'

'Thanks.' Tessa was about to replace the receiver when she heard Debbie say, 'I'd better leave Keith a note or he'll go beserk.'

CHAPTER SIXTEEN

'I don't consider it a good morning so you can stop looking so cheerful' growled Chief Inspector Fowler, ignoring Detective Sergeant Branch's greeting. A visiting cousin, a new restaurant and highly spiced food had resulted in indigestion and a restless night.

Branch's expression became sombre and in a quiet voice he said 'Inspector Kershaw would like a word, as soon as possible.'

'Tell him to come along. Let's hope it's good news.'

Kershaw looked grim and his greeting was brief as he seated himself opposite the Chief Inspector.. 'This isn't relevant to the antiques investigation however I think you should hear it.'

'Very well, as long as you're not wasting my time.' The sound of Keith Morgan's voice and his demand for £5,000 immediately held Fowler's attention, his eyes glinted angrily at Keith's reference to Jessica's death and he was momentarily speechless at Keith's choice of expletives.

'Morgan sounds a nasty piece of work. Is he responsible for his cousin's death?' asked Kershaw while Branch was still blinking and open-mouthed.

'He's one of our suspects' and then, as Branch started spluttering, Fowler demanded, 'Come on man, out with it. What's bothering you?'

'Debbie Ashe. If she went back there last night the chances are that he's knocked her about.'

'Debbie struck me as the sort who can defend herself,' interrupted Fowler. 'And she probably left again.'

'I'm sure Tessa Ormerod must have been upset' said Kershaw. 'I'll 'phone her when I get back to my office.'

'No. Although you're monitoring all in-coming calls this is really relevant to our case so I'll 'phone her.' Kershaw and Branch waited expectantly, listening to the one-sided conversation and watching Fowler's expression change from concern to disgust and finally relief when he said, 'Under the circumstances it was very thoughtful of you to 'phone Debbie. I'm glad to hear she stayed with a friend last night and that she's going home for a week's holiday.'

Kershaw picked up the tape. 'What do you propose to do about Keith Morgan?'

'Apart from keeping a watchful eye on him we can't do anything, however I am rather curious about his gambling debts' and as the two men nodded simultaneously, Fowler continued, 'the management at the casino would never allow anyone credit to such an extent, nor would any of the book-makers.'

'Perhaps he was making it up,' offered Branch. 'Maybe he really wants to spend the money on the house, or even anything else but thought that Tessa was more likely to pay up if the debt collectors were after him.'

'Morgan must be really desperate to get hold of some cash. Let's hope he doesn't think of stealing from his employers or anyone else. If I hear anything I'll certainly let you know.'

'Thank you for keeping us up to date.'

'Suppose ..' Branch didn't wait for Kershaw to close the door. 'Suppose Keith hasn't gone to work, he's there when Debbie arrives to ..'

Fowler didn't give Branch time to complete the sentence. 'If he is, and is still being aggressive I'm sure she'll get out of the house at once and possibly contact us.' At that moment the 'phone rang and as Fowler said 'Good morning, Miss Ashe', at the same time leaning back in his chair, Branch found himself listening to another one-sided conversation. Exclamations and, although ungrammatical, the phrase '"He's done what?" were repeated several times then, quite blandly and wearing an innocent expression, 'No, I don't know anything about Keith's 'phone call to Tessa Ormerod.'

There was another pause then Fowler nodded, 'I see. So, when you come back you'll be staying with the same friend until you find alternative accommodation but you'll give Tessa your 'phone number. If you don't mind me saying so, Miss Ashe, I think you're doing the right thing.'

'What's happened? What's Keith done?'

Aware that Branch was bursting with curiosity Fowler asked him to organise some coffee and then told him that Keith had apparently gone berserk. He had smashed every item in the kitchen within reach, with the result that the floor and all the surfaces were covered with shards of china and slivers of glass. From ceiling to floor the walls in the living room and hall had been defaced, using a red felt-tip pen he had scrawled, "BITCH. TESSA IS A BITCH, SO WAS JESSICA!" Debbie was already upset about his behaviour last night but on seeing this she decided there was only one thing to do. She packed all her belongings and left.'

'Keith must have been in a really nasty mood to do that.' Branch nodded his thanks as the constable placed their coffees on the desk. 'I suppose he went to work this morning?'

'Debbie said there was no sign of the suit he usually wears. He certainly won't be very happy this evening when he discovers she's moved out.'

'Does he know where her parents live?'

'No. Apparently he never asked or showed any interest in her family, and she didn't tell him.'

'Selfish sod!'

Tessa watched as Susan's formal greeting, 'Good afternoon, Mrs. Wingate' was quickly dismissed by Heather who held out her arms and embraced Susan, exclaiming her delight at seeing the younger woman again. It was obvious they were both eager to hear about her visit to Guernsey and Amanda.

'If it wasn't for the different hair-styles we wouldn't be able to tell you apart' commented Heather as she and Susan studied the photographs.

'That's what Hazel Maybury said when we first met on Friday evening.'

'What else did she say, did she meet your Aunt Margaret?' These questions came out in a rush then Susan looked embarrassed. 'I'm sorry. I shouldn't be so inquisitive.'

'Nonsense, you've every right to know what happened. The children were left in your care.' Heather glanced at Tessa. 'Sorry. I shouldn't have interrupted although I must admit I'm as curious as Susan.'

'They didn't meet.' Tessa briefly recounted what she had learnt from Hazel and concluded, 'She and her husband are a charming couple and, under the circumstances, Amanda couldn't have had more loving parents.'

'Will she be coming to Bristol?' asked Susan.

'Yes, but I don't know when. We've invited them to stay with us whenever they come, and her parents. Amanda is just as keen to meet you and Tim, who's a policeman and already knew about the antique robberies, wanted to know more about them and Jessica's accident.'

'Antique robberies' echoed Susan who had never watched any of the antique programmes and therefore did not know of Tessa's participation in these. It was after Tessa had explained that Susan said, 'The couple who live next door to the hotel had several valuable items stolen last autumn. It happened a fortnight after they'd appeared on one of your programmes. The police were all over the house and grounds, looking for clues or material evidence, without success. Although the couple were insured and have since had new locks fitted they're still very nervous.' Susan drank her tea unaware of Tessa's raised eye-brows and Heather shaking her head.

Although she knew that Inspector Kershaw's team would be in the area with photographs of the man she had identified, Tessa asked, 'Were there any strangers acting suspiciously before the robbery?

'We, the family that is, and all of the staff were questioned but at the time the hotel was full of golfers, all regular guests. The robbery occurred during their stay so they were also questioned. I thought the Inspector in charge, his name was Kershaw, was rather good looking and certainly very efficient.' Susan was looking at Heather and did not see Tessa grin.

'It's not very pleasant having your home burgled, possibly ransacked' said Heather.

'Although they don't own anything of great value it's made the other people in the neighbourhood rather nervous' said Susan.

Tessa nodded.'That's understandable. However, changing the subject, Tim is intrigued that Susan should find me again, that she hadn't forgotten us.'

'How could I?' Susan did not attempt to hide her indignation. 'I'll never forget the morning your aunt told me my services were no longer required. In spite of this I sent you all a birthday card each year and wrote to your aunt, asking how you were. I did this until you were five but she didn't answer any of them.' On learning that Heather and the Taylors had the same problem Susan resumed, 'They must have been even more upset. Irene always 'phoned her mother every Sunday, telling her about the children.'

Heather gazed at Tessa. 'It's a pity you never knew your grandparents. They were a homely couple, and thought you were all absolutely adorable. Because neither of them enjoyed good health Irene suggested that the christening take

116

place in Scotland but they insisted on travelling down. Obviously they were thrilled and delighted to see you but we could all tell that it was an effort.'

Susan nodded. 'I remember Irene saying it took them several weeks to recover from the return journey. '

'And we never knew them, or even anything about them until it was too late. Whenever we asked Aunt Margaret if we had any grandparents she always evaded our questions.' Tessa glanced from one to the other. 'Did they know we were split up?'

'No' said Heather softly. 'I only met them twice, at your parents' wedding and the christening. I'm sure if they'd known what Margaret was about to do they would have asked Susan to move to Scotland with the three of you.'

'Which I would have done, gladly.' Susan hesitated then, still looking at Heather, 'I realise there was no need for you to do so however, have you seen Keith since you returned?'

'No, but I have met his girl friend, Debbie' and when Tessa and Susan exclaimed, Heather elaborated, 'She introduced herself when I was at Reception yesterday morning. I noticed from her name badge that she's Head Receptionist. She's certainly very attractive and has a pleasant manner.'

'That's more than you can say about Keith' said Tessa.

'What's he ....' Susan stopped abruptly and apologised. 'I've no right to be so inquisitive.'

'As our nanny you're as entitled to know what's happening as anyone else' said Tessa and resumed, 'When we went to see him, to ask if he knew what had happened to Amanda, he thought it was about Jessica's Will. That was a week ago. He was annoyed that he hadn't heard from Mr. Harcourt, that Jessica hadn't left him anything.'

'Why should she?' asked Heather.

'Apparently she refused to lend him some money to do up the house and he obviously hoped she's included him in her Will.' Tessa paused as she refilled the cups. 'If the other rooms are in the same state as the living room, which was all we saw, the place is certainly in need of repair and redecoration. Discoloured wall paper and paintwork, faded curtains, shabby furniture and worn carpet. I know it's nice to relax in casual clothes but Keith looked a proper mess. Anyhow, that's irrelevant. I just wish the police would find the perpetrator and make an arrest.'

'Have they had any response to their appeal?' asked Heather.

'No, but it was repeated yesterday.'

CHAPTER SEVENTEEN

'That was the most sensible and informative person who's responded to our appeal' commented Chief Inspector Fowler as the door closed behind a shapely smartly-dressed brunette.

'Not bad looking, either' said Detective Sergeant Branch, aware that the Inspector was about to elaborate on what had been learnt.

'So we now know that three people were seen near Jessica's car. Gregory, who was there first, exchanged a few words with Keith then returned to the office. We don't know how long Keith was there, only that he was standing by Jessica's car when Gregory reached the corner. And finally we have a young woman who answers to Sarah's description. We know she went out to buy some cakes but not the exact time, or how long she was out. It's too late to 'phone the agency and the girls won't be home yet.' Fowler flicked through the contents of the file which was open on his desk. 'I'll 'phone Rena and Lisa before we call on Sarah.'

An hour later, after several futile attempts, Fowler immediately noted the surprise in Rena's voice and was glad that, without any hesitation, she confirmed that Gregory had returned empty-handed. She thought he was out of the office for about ten minutes. Long enough to tamper with the brakes, considered Fowler. He knew that Gregory was standing by Jessica's car when Keith drove into the empty space.

Rena then told him that the cakes had been bought from a shop which was about six doors to the left of the agency, which meant that Sarah had to cross the side road twice. Although she did not own a car and there was no apparent reason for her to do so, Sarah could easily have gone to their parking area.

Lisa's replies were also brief. She confirmed that neither Jessica, Rena, Roger or herself had left the office that afternoon and she thought Sarah was out for about ten minutes. She agreed it was only a short distance to the shop but suggested they might have been busy, that Sarah had chatted to a shop assistant or stopped to talk to someone in the street. Lisa also stated that Sarah could drive but did not own a car and concluded, 'It's probably irrelevant but Sarah is hoping to get Jessica's job.'

'And that would probably mean a nice increase in salary.' Fowler looked across at Branch. 'It's time we paid Sarah a visit.'

Chief Inspector Fowler glanced at the semi-detached house as they passed, noting the small but well-kept front garden and glass panelled front door, thinking that the Mortimers were probably a respectable hardworking couple. Then turning, he told Detective Sergeant Branch, who had parked further down the road, 'Right, off you go.'

'Aren't you coming in, sir?'

'In a minute.'

Sergeant Branch rang the bell and stood back, glancing up at the house and the adjoining one. Westbury-on-Trym was a pleasant area, not far from the Downs, the Suspension Bridge and Leigh Woods then, as the door opened and a gray-haired woman appeared he asked, 'Is Sarah ...' but got no further.

The door was pulled wide open and the woman whom he presumed to be Mrs. Mortimer called out, 'Sarah, your young man is here. You didn't say you were going out.'

'I'm not.' Nevertheless Sarah appeared at the far end of the hall and as she approached her eyes widened and she gasped, 'What are you going here?'

By now Mrs. Mortimer was alarmed and clutched Sarah's arm. 'Who is he? Shall I 'phone the police?'

'There's no need for that.' Branch swiftly produced his warrant card, 'Sarah and her colleagues at the estate agency are helping us with our enquiries into the car accident in which Jessica Bostock died. I'd like to ask her a few more questions.'

'Of course, come in' and as a tall, broad shouldered man opened the gate and came up the path Sarah exclaimed, 'Chief Inspector! Where have you come from?'

Fowler followed Branch into the narrow hall. 'Good evening Mrs. Mortimer, Sarah' and then into the lounge, 'This shouldn't take long' and a moment later declined the offer of tea or coffee.

'Where else did you go on the Friday afternoon that you went out to buy some cakes?' asked Branch.

'No .. nowhere. I bought the cakes and went straight back to work.'

Sarah had been startled by this question but almost leapt in the air when Fowler, seated in the armchair opposite hers, said, 'Aren't you forgetting something?' Then, noting her hesitation, 'You were seen near Jessica's car in the parking area behind the agency. What were you doing there?'

'Looking, just looking' and aware of the Inspector's grim expression, Sarah elaborated, 'I'm saving to buy a secondhand car. I've often admired Jessica's and would like one like that. I passed my driving test six months ago.'

'There's more to it than that' said Branch. 'Can you change a wheel?'

"Have you ever lifted the bonnet, looked inside?' This came from Fowler and caused Sarah to jump up, her eyes blazing and her lips quivering. 'Why don't you come straight out with it? You've probably suspected me ever since you knew I went out with Roger. You've possibly guessed that I'm still in love with him and you're right - I am. But we can't have everything we want and I've reconciled myself to that.

And yes, I have looked under the bonnet. It all looks very complicated however I only want to drive a car.' Sarah paused and held out her hands. 'Lisa doesn't miss a thing. She would certainly have noticed if I'd gone back with dirty oily hands and chipped nail varnish.'

'Did Heather and Susan enjoy themselves this afternoon?' Matthew thought Tessa looked troubled and wanted to distract her from whatever was worrying her.

'Yes. It was lovely to hear them talking about my parents however, after they left, I started thinking about Keith.'

'Don't waste your time doing that. He's not worth it.'

'I can't understand why he asked for £5,000 to pay off his gambling debts. It's ridiculous, he can't possibly owe anyone that amount. It's not as though Keith is someone of importance who might be allowed credit for such a huge amount.'

'That's exactly what Roger and I thought' and in reply to Tessa's enquiring look Matthew told her, 'Roger 'phoned to ask how you were and we discussed Keith. We agreed he probably used that as a ploy to get money out of you. However I suggest we have an aperitif now, a bottle of wine with our meal and an early night.'

Matthew watched Tessa slowly relax as she sipped her sherry, her eyes shining as he told her that the couple to whom she had spoken at length that morning had returned and purchased the seven inch high Meissen figure of a Malabar musician.

'That's good! They were really interested in it and I don't blame them. It's really lovely and so colourful, blue tassels, puce coat and purple trousers.'

'They also bought a pair of Royal Doulton vases.'

'Not those I've admired ever since you had them?' and when Matthew nodded, 'They're really unusual with their slender inverted baluster form and shades of purple and brown.'

'That's not all. About half past four, another couple who had been quietly browsing bought the mahogany bookcase.'

'The one with the astragal glazed doors, 18th century?'

'That's right. They looked at the other two but the wife thought the ebonised oak, Victorian, was too fussy while the mahogany bureau bookcase was too big and more than they could afford. They were just about to leave, highly delighted with their purchase, when the wife asked about you, explaining that their friends, who had bought the Meissen figure and vases, and with whom they had lunched, had spoken of your incredible knowledge of so many items in the shop.'

'You have so many lovely ...' Tessa stopped abruptly as the 'phone rang, her animated expression changing to one of consternation and Matthew wished he hadn't agreed to their incoming calls being monitored. He had already put his glass on the coffee table, ready to leap to his feet, when Tessa smiled, her whole body relaxing. 'Hello Amanda! How are you?' Within seconds her eyes were sparkling with excitement. 'Yes, that's fine. We'll look forward to seeing you both Thursday evening. Have you made an appointment to see Mr. Harcourt?'

Matthew's stomach rumbled with hunger and he decided that if this was going to be a long conversation he needed a couple of cream crackers to sustain him then Tessa was saying, 'See you on Thursday.'

'What's happening for them to be coming over so quickly?' asked Matthew a few minutes later, his plate half empty and feeling considerably better.

'Tim's off duty and as Amanda was able to re-arrange her Friday lessons, thought it would be a good idea to get things moving. He's going to 'phone Harcourt tomorrow morning.'

Matthew swallowed his last mouthful. 'That's going to be awkward, isn't it? I mean, how is he going to explain...'

'He's worked that out already' interrupted Tessa. 'He's spoken to two firms of solicitors here so he can honestly say one of them suggested he try Harcourt. There'll be no need for them to mention your encounter with Amanda or our visit to Guernsey.'

'Um .. don't you think that's deceiving the old boy?'

'No! Even if Uncle Laurence was scared of Aunt Margaret, Mr. Harcourt should have tried to find Amanda years ago. I'd certainly like to be there when she walks in. I'm sure both Mr. Harcourt and Judith will have a shock.'

'I hope it doesn't give Harcourt a heart attack.'

At the same time that this conversation was taking place Keith was standing in the middle of the kitchen, swearing profusely, uttering vulgar obscenities about Debbie and that she had not cleared the chaos created by him the previous evening. Glass and china scrunched under his feet every time he moved and after a quick glance in the 'fridge, when he saw there were only two eggs and a small piece of cheese, he walked to the bottom of the stairs and shouted 'Debbie, where in the hell are you?' Again there was no response and pulling a felt-tip pen, this was bright green, from his pocket Keith scrawled "Debbie is another Bitch!" on the wall. Standing back he viewed the scrawl of the previous evening and nodded, 'Now there's three of them. But where is she? I want my meal and something more substantial than a cheese omelette.'

After a large neat whisky and with his glass refilled Keith decided that Debbie must still be at the hotel, then swore at the telephonist who told him that Debbie was not on duty. When informed that Debbie was on holiday he refused to believe this and again used such obscene language that the duty manager severely reprimanded him, adding that his insulting remarks would immediately be reported to the police.

'Bollocks!' muttered Keith and aware of the gnawing pangs of hunger decided there was only one way to assuage this, go to the nearest pub where he knew he could get a decent meal. Fortified by another whisky Keith slammed the front door and was about to walk away from the house when a police car pulled in to the kerb, the driver got out and approached him. 'Mr. Morgan, Mr. Keith Morgan?'

'Yes' and as another uniformed policeman emerged from the front passenger seat Keith demanded, 'What's this all about? You can't harass me in the street like this.'

'You've just been reported as making an abusive 'phone call. This is your first warning.'

At this Keith became aggressive and with his hands slightly raised took a couple of paces towards the uniformed driver. But it was his colleague, a man in his mid-forties who stepped forward and said tactfully, 'I hope you have a pleasant evening, Mr. Morgan.'

'H'mph!' Surprised by this sudden change Keith stared at the two policemen, thrust his hands in his trouser pockets and proceeded along the pavement.

'Awkward blighter, how come you know him?' asked the driver.

'His mother was knocked down on a pedestrian crossing and died a few days later. I was on duty when he came to the station. He wanted to know what to do about getting compensation. He was more concerned about this than his mother's death. Then, when his father died, not very long after, his girl friend moved in. She's a good looker, works at the hotel near the Cathedral. He can't be an easy person to live him and I'm surprised she's stuck with him so long.'

'I wouldn't like to be around if he has much more to drink. Strikes me the type who could be really violent.'

'Hopefully it won't be us who are called out to deal with him. Anyhow, we'd better get back to the station.'

CHAPTER EIGHTEEN

'Damn and blast! She didn't even buy any milk, that means black coffee and no cereal.' Keith slammed the 'fridge door, the sight of the meagre contents had not improved his temper and reminded him of Debbie's absence. 'What is she doing, no shopping, only one clean shirt' complained Keith as he half filled and plugged in the kettle then, as he searched amongst the few odd cups left on the table, he saw a sheet of writing paper, folded, with his name written on it.

'She .. she can't do that, go on holiday without me' muttered Keith through clenched teeth then, as the kettle whistled, aggravating his throbbing head, he remembered that one of the hotel staff had told him Debbie was on holiday. 'The mean conniving bitch, I bet she hasn't gone alone. She's got another man. They've gone away together.' Keith spooned some coffee granules into a cup, reached for the kettle but holding it awkwardly some of the boiling water spluttered onto his hand as he added sugar. Sipping the scalding liquid he grinned, 'They won't be quite so happy when I find them' but his expression of glee quickly changed to one of disappointment as he recalled the deputy manager's reprimand. How else could he discover her whereabouts and the police warning?

Disregarding the chaos around him and underfoot Keith rubbed his chin, as though seeking a solution, at the same time feeling patches of stubble which would no doubt be noted by his employer, who was always impeccably groomed. Unfortunately he didn't have time to go upstairs to rectify this.

As he drank the remainder of his coffee Keith continued to mutter about Debbie's absence, reluctantly admitting he didn't know the names of any colleagues at the hotel, or even her parents' address, so who would know her destination? It was as he set his mug down amongst the other debris on the table that he suddenly wondered if Tessa knew. There was no reason why she should, they hardly knew one another nevertheless there was no harm in asking. He knew that Tessa arrived at the shop about ten o'clock most mornings and quickly decided to be in the vicinity at that time.

Keith found himself a few doors from Matthew's antique shop in good time, and was studying the display of books and their titles when he saw Tessa's reflection in the shop window. Spinning round he caught hold of her arm but before he could utter her name she turned her head, 'Keith, how dare you! Let go of me.'

'Tessa, I must talk to you.' Keith's grip tightened and unconsciously he raised his right hand, 'I need to know...' but as Tessa struggled to free herself another hand landed firmly on Keith's shoulder and the owner, a round-faced young man enquired, 'Are you all right, Mrs. Ormerod?'

'Yes .. yes, thank you. But how ...'

A warrant card was quickly produced, 'D.C. Small' and as Keith swore, 'This man was obviously making a nuisance of himself. Do you wish to make a complaint?' then as Tessa's eyes widened, 'Do you know him?'

'He's my cousin, Keith Morgan. I think he wanted to talk to me.'

Keith attempted to shrug off the constable's hand. 'Let go of me. Haven't you got something better to do?' then, looking at Tessa, 'Debbie's gone on holiday. Do you know where?'

Tessa glared at Keith. 'My God, you've got a nerve! Not only did you make unpleasant threats over the 'phone on Monday night, you now annoy me in the street. No, I don't know where she is, however I would like to go to work and I'm sure you should do the same. You're already late.'

'That's none of your business. I only wanted ..'

'I think you should do as Mrs. Ormerod suggested.' In spite of his youthful appearance the constable's voice was firm and turning to Tessa he said, 'I'll just walk to the shop with you.'

Disregarding curious stares from passers-by on the pavement Keith turned to walk away, at the same time muttering, 'Rich conceited bitch! One of these days she'll get her come-uppance.'

'Darling, are you sure you're all right?' asked Matthew for the umpteenth time after the constable had departed, Norman had made and Tessa drunk a cup of strong sweet tea.

'Yes, and do stop fussing.' Tessa looked up at Matthew over the rim of her cup. 'For a horrible moment I thought it was the man who 'phoned but his voice is smooth in comparison, Keith's is brash. In a flash the young constable was there, ready to manhandle Keith.'

'Thank goodness he was.' Matthew gave a deep sigh of relief. 'I'm just so grateful that you're safe. Keith's a bad-tempered sod, he could've hurt you when you said you didn't know where Debbie has gone.'

'I doubt it, there were a number of early morning shoppers around. However, as you said, the young detective was very quick but I think he was disappointed I didn't want to lodge a complaint. No doubt Inspector Kershaw, who arranged for him to watch over me, will be frustrated it was Keith and not the man who 'phoned.'

'I wish they could find the culprits responsible for these robberies and that it would all stop. I don't like you being mixed up in all this. I almost wish you hadn't been asked to join the team...'

'Oh don't say that,' interrupted Tessa. 'You know how much I enjoy it and that they're all pleased with me.'

'And quite rightly so. You're very knowledgeable about a number of antiques, you look absolutely stunning on television and I'm very proud of you.'

'Thank you, darling.' Tessa paused as she unlocked an Edwardian mahogany bow-fronted display cabinet, removed, lightly dusted and replaced a Chinese crystal snuff bottle, then another - Chinese blue and white, flask-shaped, and finally a Chinese crystal snuff bottle with an amethyst stopper. Reaching for the silver snuff box she held this gently in the palm of her hand, 'Simple but so elegant.'

'And complete with spoon' returned Matthew. 'However I would feel much happier if you put it back. I know you enjoy handling it but if for some reason you were distracted and put it down, it could easily be slipped into a small pocket.'

'Probably by a very unscrupulous character.' Tessa edged the snuff box into its former position, closed and locked the door. After a final admiring glance at the plush-lined interior, the one long drawer below, square tapering legs and spade feet Tessa handed the key to Matthew. 'This cabinet is really lovely, ideal for showing off its present contents, however could you check that it's properly locked.'

'This is certainly a morning when things happen. Although it's nothing to do with our enquiries Keith Morgan is still determined to find out where his girl friend has gone.' Inspector Kershaw had been informed of Keith's behaviour, that Tessa had been escorted to Matthew's antique shop, which was nearby, and resuming, told his sergeant, 'And now news that the man who approached Tessa was seen in Shepton Mallet prior to the robbery. Details are being fax-ed through.'

Five minutes later Kershaw nodded his thanks as the fax was handed to him and quickly noted that, although he had not been a resident, Colin and Bob Ratcliffe, joint owners

130

of a hotel in Shepton Mallet, and the barman, had recognised the man in the photograph. Colin and Bob had seen him standing in the foyer studying literature about local events while the barman had served him a gin and tonic, and a ham sandwich. With concentrated thought they had individually offered the same information, that this was two days before the burglary occurred, when the hotel was full with a party of golfers who fortunately all belonged to the same club.

Acting on her employers' instructions, who were only too pleased to assist the police, the receptionist had supplied all the addresses and arrangements were in hand for the visiting golfers to be at their club the following evening, when they would be shown copies of the photograph.

The same man had also been observed by the neighbours who lived on the other side of the house that had been burgled. They volunteered the information that, whilst he hadn't acted suspiciously - he had merely walked a short distance past their home, he had been studying the style of the houses and looking at the colourful gardens on either side of the road.

Kershaw continued to read, learning that a salesman looking out of a gents' outfitters, which was situated in the main shopping street, had also seen the same person. Again he had been alone. But a waitress in a tearoom in the same street said he had shared a table with a young tidily-dressed woman who was unknown to her and the other staff. They had been busy, all tables taken and the conversation between the two unknown customers might have been cursory.

Copies of the photograph had been sent to police stations in the areas where other burglaries had occurred and by mid-morning Kershaw was still reading faxes but it was one from Bath which held his attention. It related to the burglary of a large house on the outskirts of the city three months ago. Whilst the owners, who had taken some of their family heirlooms to the antique roadshow the previous autumn, did not recognise the man in the photograph a neighbour stated that she had seen him four weeks before the burglary.

Mrs. Parfitt, a retired teacher who occupied the ground floor flat in the house opposite that burgled, was positive about this. She had been recovering from an operation and walked in the public gardens almost opposite her flat twice a day and, each morning, always at the same time, she had seen him walking with a younger woman, their arms around each other. They had kept to the part of the gardens from which there were good views of the house, stopping now and again, ostensibly to examine the shrubs and trees between the path and the boundary wall.

'So, despite the numerous faxes, Shepton Mallet and Bath are the only two places where they've been seen together and while we've a photograph of him we've nothing of her.' Kershaw was seated in Fowler's office and watched as the Chief Inspector tapped the fax from Bath. 'This Mrs. Parfitt is very articulate in her description and obviously very co-operative so I suggest you arrange for an identikit to be done this afternoon. Send that young constable who was on the spot when Morgan scared Tessa, Tom Small. He's a bright young man and might come back with some useful information.'

Kershaw nodded. Although he was in charge of these investigations Chief Inspector Fowler was masterminding them and he gloomily reflected that there was usually a month between the burglaries, so there could be another one at any time.

Meanwhile, in another part of Bristol, Heather and Arthur exchanged glances as Douglas Harcourt blustered that he had not yet done anything about tracing Amanda. He had been too busy.

'That's not good enough.' Once again Arthur's expression was grim and his voice icy. 'When we left you on Friday, you said you would contact the Salvation Army, you have all the details. If you were so busy surely your secretary could have made the necessary call. You are the senior partner in this practice and I don't think you're behaving in a very professional manner.'

'The truth is that you've no genuine excuse' interrupted Heather. 'You know how much Tessa would like to find Amanda, why don't you just get on with it, or is there something else you didn't tell us? We know the bank account in her name is in order.'

'Really Mrs. Wingate! You surely didn't think ...' Harcourt broke off as there was a gentle tap at the door and Judith stood in the doorway. 'I'm sorry to interrupt. There's a Mr. Lockwood on the 'phone. He's calling from Guernsey in the Channel Islands. I've made an appointment for him and his wife to see you on Friday morning.'

'Why are you telling me this? You always make all my appointments, what's so different about this?'

'Mr. Lockwood wants to talk to you about the late Mr. and Mrs. Gilmour-Morgan.'

'Who are these people? How do they know I handled Richard's legal affairs?' demanded Harcourt and while Judith explained that another firm of solicitors had suggested Harcourt, Gunnersby and Simmonds, Arthur squeezed Heather's hand.

Judith glanced at the Wingates and back to Douglas. 'I realise this isn't very ethical, however I thought Mr. or Mrs. Wingate might remember the Lockwoods if they were all friends of the Gilmour-Morgans.'

Harcourt swung round and addressing Heather, asked, 'In spite of it being a long time ago, can you remember anyone of that name?'

Heather shook her head. 'No, however aren't you forgetting the conversation we've just had, that we would like you to trace and find Amanda. Why can't you make the necessary 'phone call now, give them the necessary details then I can return to the hotel assured that some action is being taken.'

Keith slammed the front door and swore. Everything had gone wrong since he got up and hell, there was still no milk or food in the house. Debbie had always done the shopping, ensured that he had a clean shirt and now he didn't even have that. His encounter with Tessa had been futile, his boss had been bad-tempered and his potential customer, who he had driven to Weston-super-Mare and who had driven back, was uncertain as to whether he really wanted a Rover.

In the tiny utility room Keith looked at the washing machine and reasoned that it shouldn't be difficult to operate. All he had to do was put the dirty clothes in, fill the right compartment with powder and push a couple of buttons - he'd then have a clean shirt for the morning.

Dressed in jeans and t-shirt, the washing bundled together, Keith looked around the bedroom and suddenly realising there were none of Debbie's cosmetics or little ornaments on the dressing-table, he pulled open the drawers and wardrobe door to discover they were empty. All her clothes and belongings had gone. 'Damn and blast!' exploded Keith. 'She's not on holiday, she's left me.'

Back downstairs Keith stared at the 'phone, again realising that he knew very little about Debbie's life before they met. Every time she mentioned a happy childhood and her parents he had not bothered to listen and therefore had no idea where her parents lived. It was possible Tessa knew but after her adamant response that morning he didn't feel inclined to 'phone her. It was then he remembered the young plain-clothed constable had called her by name and he muttered, 'How did he know that?'

CHAPTER NINETEEN

Inspector Kershaw sighed, whilst he was grateful for all the help Mrs. Parfitt had given them he hoped she had now remembered something worthwhile. To his amazement her first words were, 'I've seen them again, Inspector. Both of them, together. I'm in Midsomer Norton staying with my cousin for a few days.'

There was a brief pause when Kershaw quickly asked, 'Is this relevant?'

'Yes, and I'll be as brief and quick as possible. We were attending a coffee morning in aid of charity at a Georgian mansion on the outskirts of the town, which is owned by a wealthy American couple, when I saw them. Again they were acting like a honeymoon couple but I couldn't help noticing their eyes were everywhere, on the collections of ivory-white Italian figurines and jade miniatures. Later, when we went for a pub lunch they were there and again I could only watch, - Enid is noted for her loud voice. Returning from the ladies I had to pass the public 'phone box. He was in there, gesticulating, the door was ajar, and whilst pausing to study a wall map I heard him say, "There's some really beautiful pieces in the house we visited this morning, and in the other two places we've seen in this vicinity." That's when I moved away.'

Once again Kershaw interrupted. 'What are you trying to tell me, Mrs. Parfitt?'

'Enid has seen this so-called honeymoon couple at various charity events held in similar private houses and, on each occasion, she noticed that they were very interested in any antiques. They're staying at the main local hotel but obviously I don't know their name.'

'That's doesn't matter, Mrs. Parfitt. You've been very helpful. Thank you very much.'

'It's all very well being generous to those less fortunate but opening your home to the general public is asking for trouble,' commented Chief Inspector Fowler. 'Especially if they own valuable or priceless antiques that are easily transportable.'

Since Mrs. Parfitt's call it had been confirmed by the hotel receptionist that the couple, who were registered as Mr. and Mrs. Smith, were the same couple who had been seen in Shepton Mallet and Bath. Kershaw then passed the same remark as Mrs. Parfitt, that the burglaries had usually taken place on a Friday night but added, 'I'll have some men watching the place and, as previously discussed, ready to follow the intruders hoping they'll lead us to whoever is behind these burglaries.'

'Oh, although it's only a few days since we left Guernsey, it's lovely to see you again!' Tessa hugged Amanda and then held her at arm's length, 'you've had your hair cut, and it's like looking in a mirror.'

Tim and Matthew exchanged amused glances but it was the former who said, 'You'd certainly create problems if you both wore identical outfits.'

It was later, as they sat round the dining table, that Amanda and Tim learnt of Keith's 'phone call, the chaos he had created in the house, unjustifiable action towards Tessa and the constable's timely intervention.

Tim then enquired if any progress had been made regarding the antique robberies and heard that, as a result of the photographs which were being shown to members of the public, Inspector Kershaw had received fresh information.

Tessa leant forward. 'It transpires that the woman who recalled seeing him in Bath, has seen him again, with the same young woman, in Midsomer Norton, where she's staying with her cousin.'

'What's Inspector Kershaw planning to do?'

'I don't know and I doubt that he'd tell me. However,' Tessa turned to look at Amanda and then back to Tim, 'I hope you don't mind, I told him that my newly-found sister was coming to stay for the week-end.'

'I realise Bristol is a large city and it's highly unlikely, but what should I do if anyone thinks I'm you and starts talking to me?' asked Amanda.

'As you'll be with Tim it's doubtful, otherwise just chat briefly and make the excuse that you have an appointment.'

As Amanda began talking to Matthew about antiques Tim turned to Tessa and, on learning that she didn't have a copy of the photograph that was being circulated, he asked quietly, 'What does this man look like?'

'About 5'10", medium build, thin features. He has light brown hair, muddy brown eyes, smooth eyebrows and a weak chin. He's well spoken, and there's no accent or trace of dialect' said Tessa. 'However, as he was last seen in Midsomer Norton I doubt that you'll....' then, as the 'phone rang, her expression changed and she sprang to her feet, while Matthew pushed back his chair. After a moment Tessa nodded in Matthew's direction and said, 'You can't go on like this Roger, coping with the agency and Gregory's unbalanced behaviour. Come round and talk to us about it' and just before replacing the receiver, 'Have you had a proper meal today?'

'What's happened?' enquired Matthew as Tessa started picking up the plates from the table and Amanda stood up to help her.

'Roger didn't go into details but it's obvious he's worried about Gregory and the agency. He would like to talk to you about it.'

'Gregory may require medical treatment or even psychiatric advice' offered Tim who had heard about Gregory when Tessa and Matthew were in Guernsey.

'Tessa?' Roger looked at the two sisters as, having heard his voice, they emerged from the kitchen together and watched as Roger, looking completely bewildered turned to Matthew who said, 'Amanda's changed her hair-style, had it cut so now I can't tell the difference.'

Amanda moved further into the dining-room, placed the sweet dishes on the table and moved towards Roger. 'I'm Amanda and I'm sorry to cause this confusion.'

'There's no need to apologise' and ignoring her outstretched hand Roger held out his arms and hugged her. 'I'm delighted to meet you. Welcome to Bristol!' and studying her face intently, he muttered 'My God! If Jessica were here and you were all wearing the same outfits then it really would be confusing. As it is you're wearing a blouse and skirt while Tessa's wearing a dress so I won't make any more mistakes this evening.'

Matthew waited until Roger had eaten the salad which Tessa had quickly prepared, and they had all been served with lemon meringue pie before asking, 'How's Gregory? Is he still coming in to the agency?'

'Yes, to your first question but he doesn't stay long. He greets the girls but I don't think he really sees them and in answer to any of my queries tells me I'm more than capable of dealing with them. He then drives off in his car,' Roger paused, aware that everyone was waiting expectantly, 'to the roadside car park at Chew Valley Lake. He sits there all day.'

Tessa turned to Matthew, her lips formed to ask 'why' but it was Tim who spoke. 'How do you know?'

'The couple, Mr. and Mrs. Baker, who ...' Roger took a deep breath, 'bought the house, 'phoned me. They met Gregory on the first occasion they came to the agency, and are concerned that he's spent the last three days, in fact he stays there until almost eight o'clock, just sitting in his car. And he hasn't been back to his own place for the last two nights. I've 'phoned about ten o'clock, left a message on his answering machine each night but he doesn't refer to them in the morning. I gather that his neighbour hasn't seen him since Tuesday. Rena, well the three girls are all concerned about him, worried about the future of the agency and their jobs.'

Roger paused to eat his lemon meringue pie then, in reply to Matthew's query about Gregory's state of health, told him, 'I don't think he's eating, his clothes just hang on him. He certainly doesn't take any interest in his appearance and today he looked terrible. Pale, gaunt and unshaven. When I suggested he should see his doctor he told me to mind my own business but he can't go on like this. Unfortunately he doesn't have any family. His parents are dead, he was an only child and, to my knowledge, he doesn't have any close friends.'

'It's not doing him any good just looking at that expanse of water all day.' Tim knew that the hill on which Jessica's accident had occurred was on the way to the reservoir and suddenly asked, 'Is he suicidal?'

'He's obviously very depressed but whether he would ever contemplate that I wouldn't like to say' replied Roger.

'Have the police been harassing him?'

Tessa gazed at Tim with admiration and Amanda whispered, 'Tim's brilliant at interrogation, isn't he?' while Matthew's eyes darted from one to the other.

'No, but Fowler 'phoned the agency this afternoon, enquiring if I knew where he was.'

'Did you tell him?' This came from Matthew.

'Only that Gregory would probably be home this evening. However, returning to the agency, I've had an idea and would like your opinion.' Roger looked directly at

Matthew and continued, 'Unless Gregory pulls himself together it seems sensible that I take complete charge. I could either buy the business or become a partner when Gregory could remain as a sleeping partner. Rena would remain as secretary and while I would advertise for a replacement for Jessica,' Roger flinched as he said this 'and Sarah, who's been very keen for some time, would take the prospective clients out to the different properties.'

'Obviously you'll advertise' said Tessa.

'Yes, but not until Monday. I'm seeing Christoper, who I've known for several years, tomorrow morning. He's in his mid thirties, reliable, enthusiastic and is a property negotiator with a well-known company.' Roger then explained that Christopher Jones had also known Jessica, had 'phoned him every week since the accident and intimated that, if and when there was a suitable vacancy, he was ready to make a change.

'It sounds as though you'd have a good team' said Matthew. 'Good luck!'

'Thanks for listening. I only hope Gregory will be reasonable and agree.'

'I wonder why the Chief Inspector is so anxious to see him?' said Tessa.

'Maybe some new incriminating evidence has been found.' Tim looked at Roger. 'I'm sure he'll advise you as soon as an arrest is made.'

141

CHAPTER TWENTY

'Tessa!' gasped Douglas Harcourt, flabbergasted and holding on to the edge of his desk, staring at Tim and Amanda Lockwood as they crossed his office, ignoring his exclamation.

'It's very good of you to see us at such short notice' said Tim.

Douglas shook the outstretched hand, wincing at the strong grip but still unable to tear his gaze from the copper curls and sapphire-blue eyes. 'Please .. please take a seat and tell me how I can help you.' Douglas watched as the attractive young woman, whom he had thought to be Tessa Ormerod, placed an envelope on the desk in front of him. The next minute he was staring at a Birth Certificate in the name of Amanda, daughter of Irene and Richard Gilmour-Morgan and dimly he heard her say, 'I understand you dealt with my parents' legal affairs.'

'You're ...'Douglas was aware of the blood pounding in his head and the young man jumping to his feet, opening the door and asking for a glass of water. At that moment Judith appeared, saw Douglas' white face through the open doorway and rushed towards him. 'Darling! What's the matter? Are you in pain?' Then looking up she demanded, 'What have you done to him now, Tessa?'

Amanda straightened and relinquishing Douglas' wrist said quietly, 'Mr. Harcourt's pulse is slightly irregular however I'm sure that he'll be fine if he's left quiet for a few minutes.' And aware of Judith's intense gaze, 'I'm Amanda Lockwood from Guernsey.'

'But ...' Judith glanced at the now open Birth Certificate and then stared at Amanda however it was Douglas who said, 'Do you know you have, or rather had two sisters?' and accepting the proffered glass and quickly gulping the contents, 'You were triplets.' Then, without giving Amanda, who was staring at him wide-eyed, a chance to reply, 'I really thought you were Tessa. This really is a coincidence, Tessa's only recently learnt that there were three of you and asked me to trace you.' Douglas looked shamefaced. 'I must admit I've been very lax about it. We did contact the Salvation Army, who are supposed to be the best people to achieve this, yesterday.'

Douglas broke off to remove Judith's hand from his arm, told her to stop fussing and with a meaningful glance, to do what was necessary and that he was now feeling fine.

'You said I had two sisters, mentioned Tessa but what happened to the other one?' asked Amanda as the door closed behind Judith.

'Jessica.' Douglas looked from one to the other and coughed nervously, 'I'm sorry to say she died as a result of a car accident. There was something wrong with the brakes. I understand the police are making enquiries. However, it's my pleasure to give you this.' Douglas extracted a bank statement from the open file and handed this to Amanda who looked at the balance and gasped.

'These accounts, there was one for each of you, were opened by Heather Wingate, Jessica's godmother. She added to them each Christmas and birthday. Jessica and Tessa were ecstatic when, at the age of eighteen, I advised them about these accounts. They immediately started looking for a flat. If you take your Birth Certificate, any adoption papers you may have, Marriage Certificate if you brought it, and the letter I'll give you in a moment, to the bank, you can then make whatever arrangements you wish regarding the account. There's also the legacy left to you by your maternal grandparents who lived in Scotland. Jessica and Tessa received theirs when they were twenty-one.' Douglas had sounded brisk and business-like but now coughed and looked away for a moment. 'I realise I should have tried to trace you as soon as I knew you'd been adopted. Margaret Morgan was a hard woman, never told Laurence what she had done, and I felt very sorry for him.'

'That's no excuse, that's a dereliction of duty' pointed out Tim and continued, 'and, as a lawyer you must be aware of that. Jessica and Tessa obviously grew up thinking they were a twin and missed the love and companionship of their sister.'

'Margaret couldn't have coped with three ...' Douglas' voice faded to a whisper and nodding to himself, 'but they could have moved to Richard's house, it would have been large enough for all of them, and retained the nanny. It wasn't a question of money, Richard had taken out insurance to cover day to day requirements, and their education. However, for some reason, that didn't happen. Laurence was worried about the third baby: one day she was in the nanny's care and then, the next day, the nanny had gone and two babies were installed in his house. Although he asked her repeatedly Margaret never told him what she had done, how she had arranged it so quickly and my apathy is inexcusable. I know it will be a shock for Tessa but ...'

It was at this point that Amanda said quietly, 'There's something you should know,. I have met Tessa. I'm sorry there wasn't an opportunity to tell you about this earlier.'

Douglas' startled gaze travelled from Amanda to Tim then back again. 'When? How? Why didn't you tell me when you arrived?' Then, with his equilibrium restored, Douglas agreed they had discussed other aspects and merely repeated, 'How?'

Amanda glanced at Tim who succintly recounted her encounter with Matthew in Exeter, and Tessa's and Matthew's visit to Guernsey.

'We both felt a certain frisson at our first meeting' said Amanda. 'The four moles on my arm were exactly as

144

described by our nanny and Hazel, my adoptive mother, supplied other relevant details.'

Douglas' eyes gleamed. 'Well, my dear, I must say I'm delighted ....'

'Not so fast,' interrupted Tim. 'If you had started making enquiries after the deaths of Margaret and Laurence Morgan, Amanda would have met and known Jessica. They could all have spent some time together.'

'If circumstances had been different the balance on that bank account would have been very useful for training college or university, however Hazel and Bruce have been marvellous,' said Amanda.

'And as for the legacy that Amanda should have inherited at the age of twenty-one ...' Tim's voice faded but his expression was forbidding.

'I know, - I was also very lax about that.' Douglas shuddered. 'How can I atone for my negligence?'

'I think that's up to you, Mr. Harcourt. What do your partners think?' Tim glanced at Amanda and they both stood up. 'Possibly you will want to discuss the matter with them.'

'Good morning, Mrs.Ormerod. I'm surprised to see you looking in another antique shop window. Is there anything in particular that you like?' Amanda turned to look at the thin-featured man who had appeared at her side. 'No doubt your husband is working but I'm glad you've found some congenial company.'

Aware that Tim was ostensibly gazing at a pair of Staffordshire ornaments in the window Amanda bit her lip, she had noticed that Tessa did this but before she could speak the man lowered his voice. 'Have you considered my proposition, Mrs. Ormerod?'

Amanda hesitated, knowing that this would give Tim even more time to study the speaker. They knew about the 'phone call and Tessa's visit to the police station and Amanda said eventually, 'I'm .. I'm thinking about it.'

'I hope you won't take too long. Perhaps your friend might be able to persuade you.' Then, in an insinuating manner, 'Does Mr. Ormerod know your companion, where you are?' and when there was no immediate reply, 'I must go. I'll be in touch within the next few days. However, you'd be wise to co-operate.'

'Phew! I couldn't have kept that up much longer' said Amanda as soon as they were alone.

'There's certainly no doubting his identity and I'm sure Inspector Kershaw would likc to know his present whereabouts.' Tim had noted the name of the street, taken his mobile 'phone from his pocket and was already punching out the number that Tessa had given him.

'You were fantastic' said Tim two minutes later, 'and the Inspector is very grateful.'

'I hope they find him.' Amanda shivered, assured Tim that she was fine but agreed that a cup of coffee would be very welcome.

'I know you don't like heights but I would like to walk to the other side' said Tim later in the day, as they stood looking across to Leigh Woods and admiring the Clifton Suspension Bridge.

'Just a little way' agreed Amanda but impressed by the view of the Avon Gorge and with Tim's arm around her waist, she walked half way across the bridge.

Later, as they slowly made their way across the Downs towards Henleaze, Tim's thoughts were of their encounter outside the antique shop that morning. He had been as surprised as Amanda that they should have met the man in whom Inspector Kershaw was so interested and who was supposed to be in Midsomer Norton, wondered if he had been found and, whilst he knew it was impossible, wished he was involved.

'That man has been there all the morning and is still there.' Mavis Baker turned away from the window, 'I wish he'd go away. This is Friday, the fourth day he's been there and I keep thinking he's watching this house and us.'

Harold scowled. 'That's ridiculous. 'We're not doing anything for him to see and there's no reason for you to be scared. Besides, although he doesn't look as smart as he did on the only occasion we met him, we know he's Gregory Niven from the estate agency. He's only sitting there, gazing at the reservoir.' Harold moved across the room to a mahogany bow-fronted display cabinet, re-positioned the porcelain figurines and then adjusted a large landscape hung on the back wall of the room, at the same time commenting, 'This is a lovely painting, one I wouldn't mind keeping but having told Smith that we'll spend the money he's paying us to live here on my going private for my hip replacement, I can't change my mind. In any case, he told us that painting is earmarked for one of their discriminating clients.'

'That's another thing' said Mavis. 'There's a delivery tomorrow morning. What if Gregory is there when they arrive?'

'Stop fussing and remember that we've only recently moved in. It's quite normal for us to have additional items delivered.'

'In a dirty unmarked van? I'm going to complain, ask for him to be moved on.'

'Oh don't be so stupid, Mavis! Who are you going to 'phone?'

'That nice young sergeant who we met on the day of the accident. What was his name .. Hedges?' Mavis frowned as she reached for the directory, 'No, it's Branch' and as she dialed, 'He's got such a nice polite manner. I'm sure Gregory won't take umbrage.'

'I still don't like it. I don't want this sergeant, or any of his colleagues in the house poking around. The extra cash comes in very useful. You could be stirring up a hornet's nest.'

'Who was that and why are you looking so pleased?'

'Mrs. Baker. You remember, they bought the house overlooking Chew Valley Lake. We met them at the time of Jessica's accident.' Branch picked up his jacket, aware that the Chief Inspector was watching him. 'Apparently Gregory Niven has been sitting in his car in the parking area opposite their house for the past three days, and he's there again today.'

'Niven's been there for the last three days!' echoed Fowler. 'Surely someone, other than the Bakers, must have known where he was?' and as Branch shrugged, 'Who are you taking with you? We don't know what frame of mind he's in and you can't bring him in on your own. I know Tom Small is on the antique team however, ask Kershaw if he can spare him.'

Half an hour later, as they approached the lake, Tom said, 'There's no cars here now.'

'Damn!' Branch checked the road and as there was no oncoming traffic, turned right and into the drive. 'I hope this Baker woman didn't come out and tell him to clear off.'

'Do come in, Sergeant, and your young companion. Unfortunately, as you can see for yourself, he's gone. Only a few minutes ago.' The front door had opened as soon as the car stopped and Mrs. Baker was apologetic, and also in a state of nervous excitement as she ushered them into the spacious lounge.

Harold Baker looked up from his copy of The Telegraph. 'I'm afraid you've had a wasted journey, Sergeant. I told Mavis not to bother you.'

'I'm sure you'd both enjoy a cup of tea after your unnecessary journey. It's freshly made.'

'Thank you, Mrs. Baker. That's very kind of you.' Branch seated himself on a three-seater chintz-covered settee, accepted the proffered cup and saucer, helped himself to what proved to be a soggy digestive biscuit and it was a moment later that he resumed. 'I realise thirty to forty minutes elapsed between your call and our arrival, Mrs. Baker, however did you see Mr. Niven drive away, notice which he went?'

Although hidden by his newspaper it was Harold Baker who answered. 'Good Heaveans, Sergeant! It was bad enough that Niven was parked there, getting on my wife's nerves. Surely you didn't expect her to watch him all the time?'

'Of course not. Like you, we're concerned about him but we won't take up any more of your time. Thank you for 'phoning us, and the tea.'

Mavis Baker rose to her feet as the two detectives stood and, ignoring Harold's frown, followed them across the room and asked, 'Do you know the cause of Jessica's accident? We were so sorry for her husband, she was such a lovely person and so helpful.'

'Enquiries are still being made' said Branch. 'However we must be on our way.'

'That was a waste of time' said Branch as he drove back towards Bristol and glancing at Tom, who was studying a printed list, 'So why are you looking so cheerful?'

'I realise we don't know where Gregory has gone but we have found ...'

'What on earth are you talking about?' interrupted Branch.

'Missing antiques.' Tom grinned. 'We were all issued with a list of items which have been stolen since the burglaries began and there were several items in the house we just visited.'

'You're joking.' Branch swerved and was glad the road was clear. 'How could you possibly tell? You were too busy drinking tea and eating ginger nut biscuits to see anything else.'

'I was merely observant when we arrived and left. In any case there is a detailed description of each item on this list.'

'So what was in the Baker's house and, more important, how did these valuable antiques get there?'

'There was a painting, two pieces of furniture and some figurines in the lounge, and an oak coffer in the hall. As to your second question, I don't know but I hardly imagine that the Bakers were the burglars. I noticed he winced every time he moved his legs and the joints on his fingers were misshapen so he's probably full of arthritis and rheumatism, while I doubt she has the strength to lift the tea tray.'

Branch glanced sideways. 'Does that mean they bought them?'

'I doubt they could afford it. We were both sitting on the settee, did you notice how worn it and the chairs were? The carpet was faded and the curtains thin.'

'My God! You don't miss much, do you?' said Branch.

Within minutes of their arrival at the station, Inspector Kershaw had been summoned to Fowler's office where they were both eager to hear about the visit to the Baker's home. 'I'm sorry that Gregory Niven had already left however I'm sure you'll be interested in what Tom has to say' said Branch.

The young constable looked embarrassed then, with his copy of the printed list on the desk, he told the two superior officers of the large landscape, the fine pair of Chippendale tables, and porcelain figurines in the display cabinet. Unaware of the exchanged glances and Fowler's raised eye-brows Tom continued, 'Then there was this lovely old oak coffer in the hall. It's a real beauty with two front carved panels.'

'You're not only observant you're quite knowledgeable about antiques' commented Kershaw.

'I've always been interested. My Gran had an old house full of lovely old furniture. However, may I continue?'

Fowler and Kershaw nodded, both keen to hear what this enthusiastic young contable was about to impart. 'As we drove back it occurred to me that there could be other items in different parts of the house. I doubt that, even as stolen goods, the Bakers could afford to buy them so maybe they're looking after these items until they're delivered to whoever has bought them.'

'That sounds rather far-fetched, the Bakers being involved' commented Kershaw.

'I don't think we should ignore the idea' said Fowler. 'If you think about it, the stolen items could hardly be delivered to the purchasers in the early hours of the morning. Even if it means moving the goods twice, a 'holding' house could be the answer. It could well be that the Bakers are in need of some cash. What do you think, Branch?'

'Yes, I have to agree with what Tom has told you. And if we're going along with this theory, they're in an ideal spot. There's two fields with high hedges between them and the bungalow on the left, and a small wooded area separates them from the house on the right, so no one would see anything being delivered. What's there could have been delivered at the same time as their own furniture and there haven't been any robberies since.'

'What do you think Mr. Smith was doing in Bristol this morning when he approached Amanda?' Fowler, who had been advised of Tim's 'phone call, looked at Kershaw.

'We don't know what he had done before meeting them. He wasn't following them as they had just left Douglas Harcourt, but we do know that he eventually met the young woman with whom he had previously been seen, in a pub. And after sandwiches and a drink they retrieved his car, - the make and registration number of which has been noted, and drove back to the hotel in Midsomer Norton. They haven't been out since but I'll be informed when they do. I must say it was very fortunate that Tim Lockwood was with Amanda, and that he 'phoned us immediately. However, it's now a case of waiting to see if anything happens tonight.'

'Could Gregory Niven be involved with these antique robberies?'

All three senior detectives looked at Tom with amazement and Fowler shook his head. 'No. I'd say that's highly unlikely. At the moment Niven's not capable of running the estate agency, even taking care of himself and, as he didn't go to the agency or home after leaving Chew Valley, I would like to know where he is.'

CHAPTER TWENTY-ONE

'I wonder why the Bakers moved in so quickly?' said Fowler as the door closed behind Branch and Tom and, noting Kershaw's puzzled expression, he continued, 'Just think about it. They could only look at the property from the outside on the day of Jessica's accident but viewed it several days later then, in less than three weeks they've moved in. In fact, it sounds as though they're very settled.'

'Yes, but according to Branch and young Tom the house is much too big for them and there's no way Mavis Baker, who hardly has the strength to lift a loaded tea tray or Harold Baker, who is full of rheumatism and arthritis, could cope with such a big garden.'

'Most couples of their age move into or nearer a village or town, not an isolated place like that. I often drive out that way and I must agree they have a lovely view but that doesn't compensate for the disadvantages, so why did they move out there? How did they get involved with these antique robberies?' asked Fowler.

'Roger Bostock completed the transaction, perhaps he can tell you. Shall I 'phone him?' offered Kershaw but Fowler was already punching out the numbers and talking at the same time.

'Roger has been very co-operative and informative each time I've seen him and I'm sure he'll be the same now. We know that Jessica had shown the Bakers other houses but, unless she had seen or heard something relevant, I don't see that there can be any connection between her death and the robberies.'

Kershaw watched and listened, fascinated as always by the Chief Inspector's exuberance, his explanation that his call had, unfortunately, nothing to do with the investigation into Jessica's accident and then told Roger that he would like to know more about the Bakers. 'But I don't want to come to the agency. I understand the Bakers viewed other properties before deciding on that at Chew Valley. Could you take their file home with you and I'll call in to see you later.' There was a slight pause then Fowler conceded, 'That's no problem. As this is in connection with another case I'll be bringing Inspector Kershaw with me. We should be there, traffic permitting, about five-thirty.'

After asking Kershaw to make a note of any questions he considered relevant Fowler said, 'Apparently there's a family gathering tonight. Roger has already met Amanda, the missing triplet, and her husband Tim, however the Wingates, who have just returned from Indonesia where Arthur was the U.N. Resident Representative, will also be there. Heather Wingate, who was Jessica's god-mother, is naturally anxious to meet Amanda.'

'It sounds like an interesting evening however, from the way Tim Lockwood spoke this morning, I think he's sorry he's not coming with us.'

'I'm sorry to bother you with more questions, especially at home, but this is rather important' said Fowler as he and Branch seated themselves in the two comfortable easy chairs in Roger's lounge.

Roger watched as Branch extracted his notebook then, as his gaze travelled back to Fowler, 'You said it was in connection with another case, can I just ask if it's anything to do with the antique robberies?'

'It's possible.' Fowler drank some of his tea and helped himself to a biscuit, grateful that Roger should be so thoughtful, and glanced at the file which rested on Roger's knee. 'What can you tell us about the Bakers?'

'What do you want to know?'

Branch's pencil flew over the page as they learnt that Mavis and Harold had lived in a ground-floor flat in the Redland area of Bristol. They had viewed other properties on the outskirts of the city and Jessica was beginning to despair if she would ever find them something suitable. 'I suggested the place at Chew Valley. It had been put on our books some time ago by the niece of the previous owners. Her uncle had died, her aunt was in a residential home in Bath and she was getting fed up with keeping it clean and the garden tidy. I was surprised when Jessica told me they were keen to see the house.' Roger paused for a moment and then resumed, 'As you know I took over and was even more surprised when, after a brief viewing of the house and without a survey, they agreed to buy it. They didn't quibble or haggle about the price which the niece would have been prepared to drop in order to sell it and they were anxious to move in as soon as possible.'

Roger then told Fowler that the Bakers had followed him back to the agency, signed the necessary papers, paid the deposit and a date for completion had been agreed. He then said that he had never seen the man in the photograph and surprised Fowler by asking, 'Is he the man who 'phoned Tessa?'

However, this question was ignored as Fowler asked one of his own, 'Could you give me the Bakers' previous address, please?'

'That was quick but very successful' said Fowler some twenty minutes later.

'Do you really think this Smith put up the money for them to buy that property?' queried Kershaw, surprised that on leaving Roger the Chief Inspector had arranged for two officers to call on the Baker's new neighbours at Chew Valley.

'After what we've just learnt, yes, I do.' Between them, the couple living in the first floor flat, above Mavis and Harold Baker, told Fowler they had seen Smith visit the

155

Bakers on several occasions. When shown the photograph they had not hesitated. They both admitted they were surprised when Harold Baker told them that he was arranging to 'go private' for his hip replacement, and that they were moving out to Chew Valley. 'If the Bakers had the money surely he would have had the operation earlier' reasoned Fowler.

'And you think, as he was investing all that money in the house and Baker's operation, that Smith had a look at the property?' hazarded Kershaw.

'It's certainly possible. If the Bakers are going to be 'caretakers' of valuable, possibly priceless antiques Smith would want to ensure that they were not overlooked.'

Five minutes later the call came through that the visit to the Baker's new neighbours had not been in vain. Both couples had recognised Smith as the man who, on a bright sunny evening, had strolled along the almost-deserted parking area enjoying the view of the lake and, now and again, glancing at the surrounding country-side.

Fowler glanced at Kershaw as they waited at traffic lights, 'So we now have to wait and see what happens tonight.'

'We've had a very interesting and enjoyable day, thank you,' said Tim in reply to Matthew's enquiry and added, 'I think the Suspension Bridge is fantastic, - a marvellous feat of engineering.'

'Yes, it is. Did you go across to Leigh Woods?'

'No, only half way. Amanda wasn't very keen.'

'Neither is Tessa' and holding out a glass which contained a liberal measure of gin Matthew enquired, 'How much tonic do you like?' and handing the glass to Tim, resumed, 'I'm glad you were with Amanda this morning.'

'So am I. This Mr. Smith, as the police are calling him, really thought she was Tessa and, apart from a fleeting glance in my direction whilst making insinuating remarks, he didn't take much notice of me.'

'I haven't met or spoken to the man but I must admit I'm not very happy about Tessa's involvement.'

'I don't blame you. As I told Inspector Kershaw, I wanted to follow him myself however I'm glad they know he's back in Midsomer Norton.' Tim had been surprised to hear from the Inspector soon after they returned and interested to know that they were expecting another antique robbery that evening but dismissing these thoughts he turned to Roger, 'How was your day?'

'Busy. Unfortunately Gregory didn't come in so the discussion I hoped to have with him didn't materialise, however Christopher Jones is very keen to join us and the girls all feel happy about this. Now I just have to wait until Monday, I doubt that Gregory will come in tomorrow, when we can discuss the situation.' And as he lifted his glass, 'Thanks for listening.'

'What are those girls doing? Surely they're ready by now' said Matthew. 'I wanted us to arrive at the restaurant before Heather and Arthur. They haven't met Uncle Ben yet.'

'It's very kind of you to arrange for us to meet so many people at such short notice' said Tim.

'That's no problem. Anyhow I'll find out if they're ready.' But before Matthew could do this the door bell rang with a persistent urgency and as soon as he opened the door Keith pushed him aside, shouting, 'I must talk to Tessa.'

'It's Keith, Tessa's cousin' murmured Roger quietly as he and Tim studied the untidy individual who stood in the doorway between the hall and the lounge.

'What d'you think you're doing, barging in here?' demanded Matthew, standing immediately behind Keith.

'I thought we were ready to go, so what's happening?'

Roger and Tim recognised the voice as Tessa's, it was slightly higher than Amanda's, but it was Amanda who stood in the hall and who, pushing past Matthew, Keith approached. 'Where's Debbie?'

'What are you talking about?'

'All I want to know is her parents' address.' Keith's voice faded as Tessa ran downstairs, his gaze darted from one to the other and he muttered, 'Oh God! There's two of you, exactly the same' and spinning round to face Matthew, 'Tell whichever is Tessa to give me Debbie's home address.'

'She can't tell you what she doesn't know, so will you please leave.'

By now Tessa had reached the hall and remaining at the bottom of the stairs she said quietly, 'I'm sorry, Keith. I really don't know Debbie's home address or anything else about her. No doubt the Personnel Manager at the hotel could tell you and now, as we're meeting some friends in town, we really must go.'

'Huh! So this is your missing sister.' Keith thrust his right hand in the back pocket of his jeans, shifted his weight from one foot to the other, his eyes darting from Tessa to Amanda and with a mocking smile he resumed, 'Hello Amanda. I'm your cousin Keith. Perhaps we can get together sometime and you can tell me where and how they found you. Anyway, it was nice meeting you.' Ignoring the others he walked to the front door and suddenly turned round, 'By the way, I hope you're not as mean as your two sisters, however it didn't do them any good. Look what happened to Jessica, - she died in a car accident and now, for some reason or other, there's a young detective hovering around Tessa. I don't know if he's following or protecting her, and I don't care. I want my Debbie!'

'Cheeky bugger!' exclaimed Matthew and Roger simultaneously as the door slammed, while Amanda glanced at Tessa.

'It seems to be one excitement after another in this house. What was that all about, or shouldn't I ask?'

'I'll tell you tomorrow when we go to see Susan. She was our nanny and lives in Shepton Mallet.'

'Shepton Mallet' echoed Tim as he belted himself in the front passenger seat of Matthew's estate car while Amanda and Tessa climbed in on either side of Roger. 'That's where one of the robberies took place and some of the locals have recognised this Mr. Smith whom we met this morning.'

'It seems as though you know almost as much as our police' said Matthew but Tim was thinking of the men who would be patiently waiting for the burglars to force an entry, and hoping that an arrest would be made the following morning.

On arrival at the restaurant Tessa and Matthew had noticed that Arthur and Tim were soon engaged in a lively conversation and now, seated at an oval-shaped table, Tessa was not surprised to see that Tim was engrossed in whatever Arthur was saying. She recalled that on meeting Arthur she had been interested to hear about the countries where he and Heather had lived, intrigued to learn of the culture and customs. Turning her head slightly she heard Tim say, 'Katmandu sounds fascinating. How long were you there?'

'Four years. After that we were in Bangkok, then Indonesia.'

'But I thought you flew back from Kuala Lumpur?'

'Yes. We spent a few days in Penang.'

'That's an island off the Malaysian coast, isn't it?' and when Arthur nodded Tim said, 'I think the Far East should be the destination of our next holiday. All these places you've described sound so interesting and exotic.'

'It's certainly a very different way of life. You would be surprised at some of the places and the conditions under which some of these people live.' Arthur paused, remembering the occasions Heather had wished that Amanda, Tessa and Jessica could join them for a holiday. Despite her disappointment that Margaret Morgan had ignored her letter suggesting that the girls should come to New York, once settled in Katmandu Heather had written again. Once again no reply had been forthcoming and Arthur recalled Heather crying, her vehement condemnation of Margaret. Glancing sideways at the keen, clean-cut features he told Tim, 'Let me know if you do decide to take that trip. I'm sure some of our friends would be delighted to meet you and show you around.'

'Thanks. That would be marvellous.'

Tessa noticed that Amanda's eyes were sparkling and her cheeks flushed as she told Heather and Uncle Ben about her life in Guernsey, her pupils, love of music and adoptive parents.

Ben had heard most of this when they first met in Exeter and turning to Roger, who was seated on his left, enquired about the estate agency, nodding now and again as he agreed with what Roger hoped to do.

On other side of the table Tessa took advantage of the lull in the conversation between Tim and Arthur to ask if there had been any news about the house in Wells.

Immediately Arthur's eyes lit up. 'Yes, my dear. My colleague has found a slightly smaller house in a village nearby and will be taking possession in three weeks time. They're leaving the carpets and curtains, which we both like, and our personal possessions are on the way back to England so now we can look around for whatever furniture we need.'

Meanwhile Gregory Niven was seated at a corner table in one of the village pubs with yet another glass of whisky in his hand. He had driven to Wedmore, which was set on the edge of the Somerset levels, early Tuesday evening and after finding bed and breakfast accommodation had spent the remainder of the evening, and the last two, sitting at the same table. He was vaguely aware that the landlord and regulars kept glancing in his direction and he felt sure that, in a place of this size, they probably knew where he was staying and that he drove off in the same direction every morning.

Raising his glass to his lips Gregory hazily considered that there was nothing he could do that would bring Jessica back. He'd never see her sapphire blue eyes light up with enthusiasm over new properties, her eagerness in showing them to clients and her exhilaration when they decided to buy one. It was all Roger's fault. If he had gone out to Chew Valley to meet the Bakers, Jessica would still be alive and, in time, love him again.

Gregory's hand shook as he raised his glass and, at the same time, his stomach rumbled, reminding him that he hadn't eaten since breakfast, and that was only coffee and toast. He couldn't face a cooked breakfast, in fact when did he last have a good cooked meal? Gregory was aware that all his clothes were loose and that he should start eating properly.

But more important, what was he going to do about Roger and his persistent questions?

CHAPTER TWENTY-TWO

Inspector Kershaw reached for the large mug of coffee which had been placed on his desk within seconds of his arrival, amazed that with only two hours sleep, he wasn't tired. It had been a long night and before setting out the team had unanimously expressed their hopes that their nocturnal exercise would prove successful.

Chief Inspector Fowler had been present at their final briefing, wishing them all good luck but it was obvious to Kershaw who, despite the presence of two very keen and capable sergeants, had included himself in the team, that the Chief was disappointed he wasn't coming with them.

Since Mrs. Parfitt's phone call that afternoon Kershaw and his team had been busy. Two men had driven out to Midsomer Norton in an unmarked van in order to reconnoitre the Georgian mansion, its grounds and the surrounding area, at the same time finding suitable places for those participating in the exercise to park. Advised by Mrs. Parfitt of the owner's name Kershaw had soon ascertained that photographs of the valuable items had been supplied by the owner and fed into their computer when he and Fowler discussed whether the owners should be advised about the possible robbery. They knew that the husband held a black-belt in karate and was also an able swordsman; a rapier, sabre and cavalry officer's sword had been noted by Mrs. Parfitt. In fact it had been difficult to stop her expounding about these and the fact that she had seen similar weapons in her paternal grandfather's house.

However it was the knowledge of the householder's dexterity that forced Kershaw to 'phone him. Millions of pounds worth of antiques had been stolen since this spate of burglaries began so Kershaw pointed out that, whilst it was only natural the owner would want to protect his home and possessions, he would be glad if the burglars were able to

162

make a get-away when he hoped they would lead his team to whoever was masterminding the operation.

With the owner's help Kershaw soon had a rough plan of the house, means of access, where most of the antiques were to be found and the knowledge that the main entrance could not be seen from the road. Previous robberies had taken place in the early hours of the morning but this did not deter Kershaw and they were all in their allotted positions soon after midnight.

It was just after one o'clock when two vehicles, a car and a van with dimmed sidelights, quietly approached the house and drew up outside the main entrance, when six figures emerged and crept stealthily round the house, towards the french windows. Kershaw had anticipated that this would be their means of entry and indicated that the two men with him should remain where they were. He doubted that the owner had slept, even gone to bed, listening to the slightest sound and hoped that the burglars would not incur too much damage in order to gain entry.

Within minutes Kershaw had seen two figures carrying what looked like a large painting, followed by another two with smaller articles. No sooner had they returned to the house than there was a loud crash and it was with great difficulty that Kershaw and his men remained where they were. Almost at once four people emerged, again carrying smaller items when Kershaw wondered if the owner had, in fact, rushed downstairs and injured one of the intruders then another two figures appeared, one almost carrying the other. These two made for the car when the casualty was helped into the passenger seat, the other getting into the driver's seat and immediately driving away. By using night glasses the registration numbers had been noted. Kershaw had also noted that the larger items had been loaded into the back of the van while the smaller items were placed on the back seat of the car.

As pre-arranged Kershaw's team followed in two cars while Kershaw stepped from the copse in which they had been hiding and walked quickly to the house.

'As anticipated, they've taken the landscape.' The owner drank some whisky from a cut-glass tumbler, offered Kershaw and the two officers a drink which they all declined, and named the artist. 'His work is very popular at the moment. They also took my collections of ivory white Italian figurines and jade miniatures.' Then, noting that Kershaw was looking around, 'Fortunately nothing was broken. The noise you probably heard was one of them knocking over a brass-topped table when he fell. That brought me downstairs, as they would have expected, so most of them rushed out, and the sight of me waving a walking stick which I grabbed from the hall made the one still standing haul the last one to their feet, and half-carry him out. They were both wearing balaclavas, black long-sleeved sweaters and trousers, trainers and of slight build. I suppose they were both men but it was impossible to tell.'

'Our two cars are following them, at a distance so, unless they change the number plates, hopefully by mid-day tomorrow we'll know who's behind these burglaries, arrests will have been made and then we can arrange for your antiques to be returned.' As they reached the front door Kershaw shook the proffered hand, 'Thank you for your help. I'll be in touch tomorrow morning.'

Kershaw now glanced at the information that had been phoned in, noting the round-about route which had been taken by the drivers of the van and car who had eventually turned left at the side of what appeared to be an old farmhouse. The last sign-post had been for East and West Harptree. Two members of his team, one from each car had been dropped off and sprinted down the narrow track while the cars parked further along the lane. Although the house was in complete darkness the two detectives immediately saw that the sidelights of each vehicle were still on, which enabled them to see that these had reversed into an unused barn. They then watched as a short, white-haired man using a stick and with a rucksack on his back moved slowly towards the barn. In the stillness of the early morning his words carried, 'Did you get it all?'

Only the driver of the car had emerged, his reply was muffled but the white-haired man's comment, 'You knew I wanted the Georgian silver tea service for myself. I always thought you were a fool' was audible, also 'Take this damn thing off my back. As usual there's a thermos of coffee and sandwiches. Delivery to be made as usual.'

In the meantime the drivers of the two unmarked police cars had parked in an adjacent field, separated from the farmhouse by a high hedge, and had remained there for the remainder of the night but there had been no more comings or goings. Hopeful that they would soon be on the move Kershaw drained his cup then, at the first ring, picked up the 'phone when a voice said, 'We're on our way. It looks as though we're heading for the anticipated destination.'

'Good! We're on our way. Advise us if there's any hold-up or change of direction.'

Kershaw had been relieved that there were no cars or other means of transport at the old farmhouse as the description of the recipient of the items which had been unloaded in the early hours of the morning, tallied with that of a well-known collector. He had not been seen for some time but various dealers had hinted that he was probably living in a large house, miles from anywhere enjoying, maybe gloating over all the treasures he had accumulated over the years.

They were driving through Chew Magna when Kershaw, accompanied by D.C. Small, a sergeant and driver, learnt that another team of officers had just arrived at the farmhouse. Within minutes it was reported that the production of a search warrant had gained immediate entry and, although the property was very dilapidated, every room was crammed full of priceless paintings and antiques. A number of these had immediately been recognised as having been stolen and, although the white-haired man had blustered that he was merely looking after these, the appropriate action had been taken. Officers who specialised in dealing with the theft and recovery of antiques had now taken over.

A van and car were parked at the side of the Baker's house and a large painting was being manoeuvred through the Baker's front door by two untidy-looking individuals as Inspector Kershaw, Tom Small and another officer drew up, closely followed by the other two police cars. But before anyone could alight Tom said 'That's Gregory Niven's car approaching. I recognise the registration number' when Kershaw quickly gave instructions for one of the other cars to follow Niven.

Kershaw's attention was then diverted by loud voices as the two men who had carried the painting pushed and shoved each other to get through the doorway at the same time. They were still arguing when Kershaw instructed the two officers from the other car to apprehend them. In the meantime Tom and the sergeant had stopped a couple, both dressed in black, who had come from the back of the house and before they could get into the parked car. As they came round to the front of the house the two men were being bundled into the back of a police car while Kershaw, who had been standing in the doorway talking to a belligerent Howard Baker, took one look at the limping woman and her companion and left Baker standing, open-mouthed.

At his greeting, 'Mr. Smith', the man glared at him, tried to free himself from the officer's grip, demanding that he be released and then muttered, 'How do you know my name?' Reluctant that Smith and his girl friend should travel to the station in the same car Kershaw was relieved when the officers in the first car returned, Gregory was now being discreetly followed by a unmarked police car. Still protesting Smith watched as the young woman, crying and asserting that she was innocent, was driven away.

It was ten o'clock when Tim drew up outside Susan Ratcliffe's house and as he did so the front door opened and Susan emerged, gazing intently at the two copper-haired young women who alighted from the back seat of the car. Then, looking at Tim she held out her hand, 'Tim, I'm delighted to meet you but for the moment I can't tell one from the other. Please enlighten me.' Amanda hesitated, then with a gentle push from Tessa, moved forward and introduced herself, unprepared for Susan's warm welcome, the tears in her eyes, enveloping hug and, 'Don't you look like your dear mother. Anyhow, why are we all standing out here. Come in.'

Although interested in meeting Susan Tim had been concerned that the conversation would be of Amanda's life in Guernsey and was glad when he was introduced to Doris who, after exclaiming how delighted she was to meet them all, drew him to one side. 'Tell me about Guernsey.'

To Tim's surprise Doris' questions were about the hotels, leisure amenities and other attractions available to visitors. Unaware that Amanda and Susan had stopped chatting and that they were all listening with great interest Tim told Doris that, due to its initial success, Floral Guernsey was now one of the annual events. During this period several private gardens were open to the public, all of which attracted gardening celebrities and many visitors to the island.

'Although you're not involved in tourism it sounds a delightful place and you're certainly very good at promoting the island' said Doris.

It was some time later, after Susan had asked if Tim knew about the antique robberies and he declined to comment as to what progress was being made, that Susan told Amanda and Tim, 'Do come and see me when you're next in England' then, turning to Tessa, she said, 'I would like to meet Roger. Do bring him down when the first opportunity occurs.'

Meanwhile, back in Bristol, Roger was leaning against Rena's desk, about to raise his mug of coffee to his lips when the door was flung open and Gregory, his face flushed and contorted with anger, rushed in and grabbed the lapels of Roger's jacket. 'If you need a coffee so early in the morning, drink it in your own office. Sitting out here, gossiping with the staff is no way to run the agency.'

Relieved of his mug by Rena, Roger gently removed Gregory's hands and said quietly, 'I was just relaxing for a moment, pleased that the sale of that very large property near Walton Castle has been finalised.'

'Huh! You need more than one sale to keep the agency going and I hope you don't treat your new purchasers like you have the Bakers, at Chew Valley.' Then, seeing Roger's surprised expression, Gregory continued, 'Oh come on, don't look so innocent! It's a lovely peaceful spot but, although it was much earlier this morning, I couldn't help noticing that two vehicles, a van and a car, were parked right outside the house, and the police cars. Two were stationary but the third started up and followed me as I passed, however I lost them as I came through one of the villages.'

Roger's sigh of relief went un-noticed as Gregory looked around and his mood changed. 'The desks have been moved around' and with a derisive sneer Gregory continued, 'I know what you're after. You might have been successful the first time but you're not going to get away with it now.'

'What are you talking about?'

'You! You took Jessica from me and now you're after the business.' Gregory launched himself forward again, his eyes glittering dangerously, his hands on Roger's shoulders as he shook him. 'You think you're oh so clever but you're not. Why do you think I tampered with the brakes and told you to go out to Chew Valley on that Saturday morning? You were meant to die, not Jessica. But now it's your turn.'

Gregory delivered a swift upper-cut which sent Roger reeling back against one the desks then, glancing briefly at Lisa and Sarah who were clinging to each other crying, but not noticing Rena's absence, Gregory snarled at them, 'Shut up you two and stay where you are, or you'll get the same treatment.'

'Ugh!' Two quick jabs to the solar-plexus enraged Gregory when he started punching Roger about the head, still ranting. 'Jessica loved me before you came along and with you out the way she would have done so again. She would have been grateful to me for removing you, loved me with even more passion.'

As the two men exchanged blows and swayed in the limited space, chairs were pushed over and broken. It was when Gregory reached for Roger's throat again that the door was pushed so hard that it almost bounced off the hinges and a well-built business suited figure flung itself at Gregory, grabbed him round the waist and pulled so hard that they both fell back on the floor.

'Keith! What are you doing here?' gasped Roger, his eyes streaming and blood trickling from his nose as Keith stood up, hauled Gregory to his feet and pinioned his arms behind his back.

'I saw a police car parked just up the road and thought I'd look in to make sure you were all O.K.'

'Pity you can't mind your own business. Just let go of me.'

In the next instant, although the doorway was blocked, Rena slipped back inside while Detective Sergeant Branch, with Chief Inspector Fowler standing immediately behind him, charged Gregory with premeditated murder.

'Oh, don't be so ridiculous. I really don't know what you're doing here,' and although unable to turn and face Keith, 'would you mind releasing me. And what did you think you were doing, rushing in here and attacking me?'

'We heard everything you said and saw your unprovoked attack however, before we could take any action Mr. Morgan was intent on saving Mr. Bostock.' All eyes turned to Roger who, sitting on one of the undamaged chairs, was still breathing heavily whilst Rena dabbed his scratched and bruised face and Sarah asked, 'How many for coffee?'

Taking advantage of the diverted attention, but unaware of Keith's strength, Gregory attempted to free himself however before he could do so two uniformed men appeared. At a nod from Branch they moved towards Gregory and, within seconds, escorted him to the waiting car.

'Thank goodness,' muttered the Chief Inspector. 'That's another missing link' and when Branch stared at him, he elaborated. 'Tessa found Amanda, the third triplet, we found the collector who hoarded all those stolen antiques and now, Niven has admitted that he was responsible for Jessica's death.'

About The Author

Sheila was born in Guernsey in 1931 and, except for the war years has always lived in the island. In 1940, when the islands were evacuated she went to Bristol with her mother and, after a year at St. Ursula's transferred to a sister convent, a boarding school, at Clevedon where she remained until 1946. On returning to the Island she completed her education and then spent 8 years working in a bank when her recently acquired secretarial skills were used. In 1956 Sheila, her husband and her parents took over a local hotel. Her daughter and son-in-law are now in charge of this and, although retired, she still enjoys meeting the locals and regular visitors.

Read June '07 Ann Elizabeth   , 59, 95, 96, 97, 102,
                            107, 112, #22 125,
                            129, 131 (2) 136, 142,
                            144 149, 150, 162, 16?
                            169.